Homes of Healing

2

Petrea Downs

Olwyn Harris

Reading Stones Publishing

Published by: Reading Stones Publishing
                          Helen Brown & Wendy Wood
                          www.woodwendy1982.wixsite.com/readingstones

Cover Design: Wendy Wood

For more copies contact the publisher at:

Glenburnie Homestead
212 Glenburnie Road
ROB ROY NSW 2360
Mobile: 0422 577 663
Email: hbrown19561@gmail.com

For all those who have chosen to participate in church (formal and informal) with me over the years. These experiences of family and fellowship have taught me so much about my own journey of healing, and God's heart of what an experience of home can be.

1.

She burst through the door breathless. Her heart raced as she reached for the rifle from the rack in the corner. She deftly loaded and cocked it. With a sweep of her hand across her forehead, she approached the holding-yards. The stock stirred restlessly in the still pre-dawn morning. A shadow moved. A figure scuttled behind the water-trough. She was reluctant to blow a hole through that. She knew the value of water, plus the inconvenient cost of mending what held it – in both time and money. Everything went still.

"I'm warning you! Take your leave. I have this loaded and I *will* use it." She certainly was not going to have some stranger ride off with the few dozen head of cattle she had brought in for this month's sale. She brandished her gun again. "Get going! Leave now and I'll let it go. I'll let you go."

It was quiet again, but she was not fooled. She watched every outline carefully like detecting a snake in the grass. Suddenly a figure stood up and jumped the yards and disappeared among her cattle, as they milled agitatedly. A horse rider came careering through as he slipped the rails, and in an instant the runner leaped into the saddle of the spare stockhorse the rider had in tow. They quickly cut the steers in the yard and took off. She blasted the gun. There was a screech as the rider bringing up the rear hit the dust. The other rider didn't pause but pounded on with her cattle, heading for the hills that boarded the valley of her best pasture. They were gone.

2.

Meg walked cautiously towards the fallen figure. He had dragged himself towards his horse standing by the trees, leaving a smear of blood in the dust, his shirt caking in filth. She quickly reached where he lay, standing over him. She considered his contorted face and pale lips and rolled her eyes. He reached for a pistol that had been flung to the ground and she placed her boot effortlessly on his wrist. He hardly resisted. She picked up the handgun, checked the chamber, and sighted it. A look of resignation came into his eyes. A rabbit scurried near a log and she fired the gun. The animal squealed, jumped and lay still.

She looked back at the pathetic sample of humanity at her feet and grimaced. She frisked him for other weapons, and extracted a knife from his boot, and put it in her own. She took the neckerchief from his shirt and packed it against the wound on his shoulder and tied it firmly with the scarf from around her neck. She went over and grabbed his horse and dragged him to his feet. He groaned and hobbled unable to bear weight. "I'm not going to have you dying on my place. I'm taking you to Constable Matthews. He can deal with you."

"You're not going to end this?" he whispered hoarsely.

She guessed he was not a man who did failure easily.

She was pleased he had failed now, and she rubbed it like the gravel into his wound. "You did that yourself, Mate. Cattle duffing is handled seriously in these parts." She hoisted him up on the horse and led it back to the house. She took a blanket off the shelf and laid it on the floor. She left him there, throwing him a cushion from her reading chair, and then thought the better of that and covered it with a towel. He shivered and groaned, and she grabbed another blanket from her bed and covered him. She dipped a mug of water from a bucket in the corner and held it to his lips. He sipped enough to wet his lips. She checked his wound and ripped a rag into strips and reinforced it firmly. It seeped through again and she applied another. She stared at him like a bug infesting her tomato patch. Why were things never simple?

When her neighbour arrived after daybreak, Meg brought him inside and showed him Exhibit A: the captured felon lying on her cottage floor looking like death in a blanket. He shook his head in dismay and expressed his disgust at the crime and lost stock.

"I just can't leave him here," she said, "because as soon as he possibly can, he'll make a run for it: bleeding out, sprained ankle and all. He's lost a lot of blood for a shoulder wound. I wondered if you would stay and watch him while I take the stock in by myself?"

"I'll tell what, I'll send over one of the house-maids. Then she can stay as long as you need. Are you sure you want to leave him here?"

"Well I can't take him like this… and I can't afford not to take in what head are left. I can manage them myself though. I'll talk to the Constable and Doc Mansfield and find out how they want to handle it. I'm hoping they'll come back with me and take him. Sooner he goes, the happier I'll be.".

3.

"I just don't see why you have to do it here."

"Meg, it is my recommendation. This is in the best interests of my patient."

"Well what about my interests, being the victim of cattle duffing... in broad daylight."

Constable Matthews turned to her. "You said it was before dawn. That the sun hadn't come up."

"It was light enough. Doesn't change that it was audacious and criminal. What more do you need?"

"We need this man not to die. Now if the Doctor needs your help, please accommodate him," Matthews said emphatically.

"This is a fine kettle of fish! Why should I have to undertake to resolve this man's consequences? These are outcomes of his own choosing! He is the cause of a great deal of hardship in my world."

"Well it is going to get harder if he doesn't recover. You've already confessed that you aimed your shot. You don't want to be up for a murder charge."

"Murder? You've got to be kidding me! It was self-defence! I have a right to defend what is mine."

"You were in no personal danger."

"I was protecting my own. If you think losing my property or dying of starvation is not personal, you are very much mistaken!"

"I'm just doing my job Ma'am. I'm letting you know how I read the law. You shot... and the man is now in mortal peril."

"You can tell I shot only to maim."

"How could we tell such a thing? The man lies here fighting for his life."

"Because four inches that way and I would've had him in the neck. Six inches that way and it would have landed square in his back. Either way, it would have been instantly fatal. He was riding away. I had a clear shot. You tell me that's not intentional."

The Doctor finished arranging his instruments and pulled from his bag a wire-framed mask and poured some ether into a cloth. "Hold this firm. I have to extract the bullet and clean the wound. It's properly soiled." Meg rolled her eyes and complied. She was flustered and irritated. The sale had not gone well. She had got much less per head than she had hoped. It seemed the other lots leading up to hers had done much better.

Doctor Mansfield worked systematically. And he bound the wound tightly in place. "We won't be able to move him straight away. You'll have to do the basic care that he needs until he is stronger. Then we'll organise a cart to come out and transport him."

"How long is that going to be?"

"About a week. Maybe more..."

"A week!"

"Yes. At least. You know what to do."

"What do you mean, 'I know what to do'?"

"In regards to nursing him."

"I do not appreciate the comparison to nursing my husband. This man is slime. You get rid of him as soon as you possibly can! A week is too long."

"No comparison is intended, Mrs McGregor. I'm just talking about you knowing what needs to be done. A week will be required at least, maybe more."

"When are you coming to check on him then?"

"I'll come back in a couple of days." They left after they moved him off the table and back onto the make shift swag on the floor. Constable Matthews reiterated his parting thought, that it was very important for her case that the man stayed alive.

4.

If keeping him alive was the priority for the law, for Meg it was like poking hot irons into her eye-sockets. Why should she work to save this man's life after what he had done? And now there were innuendos of premeditated murder? Why should she nurse this man with skill and see him respond and become strong, when nothing she ever did made any difference with Alistair? He had been the love of her life. She had come here with him to build a family, a home, and a dream. This had been their forever-plan and that plan had been systematically shredded. Forced to nurse someone who ambushed her resources was just another blade in the executioner's arsenal of torture – instruments killing their dream.

If it hadn't been for the support of her neighbour, she was pretty sure she would have gone under straight away. Everett was always willing to throw her a lifebuoy. Crisis after crisis he had been there. But even now it seemed she was still treading water in a whirlpool where dead weights were constantly dragging her under. She was fighting; fighting hard, but she wondered how long she could keep her nose and lips above water, to stay alive. How long would her fight to stay remain?

She held his head and gave him some broth. He seemed to growl under his breath like some sort of angry, caged dog. She stuck to the regime of applying leeches around the wound until they dropped off engorged and then salted the suture-line and irrigated it clean. She almost enjoyed the look of silent agony on his face. Conveniently the cause of his pain was that she was complying with Dr Marshall's rather odd wound-dressing instructions. Who ever heard of irrigating with salted water?

Within days the fevers were abating, and she could see the colour returning to his face. Large areas of bruising were coming out around his shoulder. She re-strapped his ankle methodically; and gradually the swelling was reducing. The doctor came regularly as promised and was satisfied with his patient's progress. He didn't give any indication as to when he would be removed; that was the Constable's jurisdiction. Instead he provided more tinctures for his fevers and gave instruction to protect the movement in his shoulder and strength in his ankle. So, she swallowed her hate and her frustration and made him move; and she didn't flinch when his face contorted as she worked his range of motion. She hoped it hurt. She made it hurt.

Initially she attended to him between chores, but when she came in and he was sitting up against the wall, she knew she would have to adjust accordingly. She didn't want to come back and find him gone. So, she demanded that he come with her as she did her chores, hobbling on a make-shift crutch she cut from a sapling, wrapping the end of it in a towel held on by strips of rag she used as bandages.

She made sure his surly, sullen face was never out of her sight. She always waited until he was exhausted before she attended to those things that required her privacy, and only occasionally resorted to securing him to the verandah if she couldn't wait. She put him to work: holding gates, raking straw, carrying buckets, oiling saddles. If he had to be here, she might as well get her pound of flesh. His limping one-handed assistance provided more help than she would ever confess out loud.

More weeks passed and she still hadn't heard from the Constable. She wrote a rather terse letter, demanding that he be removed, and she charged her neighbour with delivering it with the utmost punctuality.

As he rode off with words of reassurance, she realised something. The silent man under her supervision had hardly said a word since being there. Not a word of abuse, regret, penance, appreciation or acknowledgement. Nothing. He did what she demanded even when he obviously resented her and was clearly in pain. And the more she noticed his silence the more it perplexed her. She curiously started to wonder if he was mute. Perhaps he was dim-witted and didn't have the capacity to converse. But she watched him work her horses and he handled them well, murmuring like some horse whisperer. She remembered his swift and calculated assistance to the crime and again felt no sympathy for his position. If he chose not to talk that was his business. But perhaps to know his name, since he was here, that might be useful.

That night at dinner she served him a good portion of stew. He ate it without pause. She asked if he would like some more, and he nodded. It felt like it was the first time he had responded to her. Or perhaps it was the first time she asked a question of him directly, rather than giving curt, clipped orders at gunpoint.

"What's your name?" she asked as she gave him the second helping of stew.

He looked at her then, carefully assessing his gaoler, his nurse and the warden who cooked his meals. It had taken him a while to work out the situation, but she was one who was liberal with her talk, so he had pieced together a fair summary of what happened. He had only scattered snatches of memories from that moment he sprinted out from cover to pull down the rails, until waking up on the floor being fed rabbit-broth, visited by the doctor. He focused hard on retrieving those lost hours. Slowly it was coming back.

He spoke then and answered her question. "Ben. Benjamin Harker."

"Huh. That even sounds like a criminal's name. It would not be out of place on any bushranger's poster." She poured him his tea and he skulled it. She gathered the dishes and tipped out some warmed water to wash up and threw him the tea towel. He wiped up wordlessly.

5.

Her neighbour rode up and dismounted in front of the hut. Ben was drawing water from the well and carried the coopered wooden bucket to the verandah. Meg no longer had him tethered. There didn't seem any point. If he ran, it would save her a whole lot of bother. Ben glanced briefly at the rider who said rather tersely, "I've come to see Mistress Meg."

"Ain't my mistress," he muttered putting the bucket of water on the step. He paused and looked over towards Meg as she walked out of the stables slapping the dust from her gloves.

"Oh Everett, how good to see you," she said looking past him to her visitor. "Do you have time to stay for tea?"

He nodded and tossed the reigns to Ben. He held them for a moment then tethered the horse to the verandah rail with a roll of his eyes. He picked up the bucket and silently went to water the chooks. Everett stepped into the small hut, his tread heavy on the timber floor, and he handed Meg a letter from the constable. She read it through. It contained formal assurances that since the doctor had added his declaration as a witness that she had facilitated the prisoner's recovery well, the charges of premeditated harm were no longer a concern. And as long as the accused remained on Petrea Downs while awaiting his trial, it would be considered favourably. Whatever that meant. She hoped it meant her case for restitution would not be fobbed off. She folded the letter impatiently and put it on the sideboard.

"How are you going with all this? Are you holding up?" Everett said searching her face.

Meg smiled gratefully. He always had a considerate word. He always supported her with concern. "Exhausted." It was a relief that she didn't have to pretend.

He turned away and measured his words. "Ahh... having the convict here... I hope that this situation is not causing you too much strain?"

"Of course, it is! I'm frustrated beyond measure at the delay. It cannot be accounted for." She pointed to the letter. "Constable Matthews says that he has to stay here until the court hearing. Apparently, there is a huge backlog. He is unable to give me a time frame."

"But surely this is an imposition that you are needlessly encumbered with?"

"Yes! I totally agree. It's like they've deputised me without consent. He is the problem of the law, but they won't do anything about it. The doctor says he still needs more recovery time and that would not happen appropriately in an overcrowded gaol, so he was applying pressure to Matthews for this delay as well."

"What is the point of nursing a man destined for the gallows?"

"Exactly. Or at least solid prison time." Still her

conscience told her 'humanity is humanity'. She had made her decision to comply with Matthews' expectations, and the pay-off was that her workload was easier to manage with him here. She just wasn't going to let on that this might be to her advantage in some small way.

"Why do you no longer have him secured? He could escape. For him to get away after what he did, that is unthinkable," Everett's voice was rising, incensed by the injustice of the situation.

Meg sat the teapot on the trivet to draw and collected the cups. She arranged them carefully at the table. "Everett, if you could exert some influence to speed up the process, I would be so grateful. But just now, let's enjoy our tea. I don't want to spend our time talking about petty criminals."

"Petty? I hardly call what was done at all petty!"

Meg paused. She didn't need him to be enraged for her. She had enough rage of her own. "Sugar?"

He seemed distracted and didn't answer so she pushed the small tray holding the bowl and jug over for his use. He seemed to gather himself. "Oh. Two sugars thanks."

"The bowl is just there... at your convenience."

He glanced up his eyes firing hot in annoyance. She had turned away to gather some plates from the hutch, and he quickly smoothed his brow, and spooned the sugar wordlessly into his cup, as she sat down opposite him.

Meg looked out the window and saw Ben walking up from the shed with the axe over his shoulder. He limped when he was tired at the end of a long day and it was only then that she noticed he favoured his shoulder as well. He was pedantic about grinding the axe-edge sharp. Funny that, until now, she hadn't realised she didn't actually feel unsafe with him here. The man was one ball of anger, which fuelled his work like an unstoppable machine. But his obstinate stance was more relentless, than dangerous. Regardless of the task, Ben was pushing to go further: just do 'one more' before sundown. Because she would never concede to him or allow him to out-do her, she matched him blow for blow until they were both ready to collapse from exhaustion.

Everett had not been around for afternoon tea for a while: the weekly ritual was one she looked forward to. Perhaps his insistence on having news from the magistrate before he came explained the delay. She refocused and turned to pour his tea.

"Meg I spoke to the judge on your behalf again. I tried to get him to see the unreasonable position that you have been placed in, of course. But the man swears that he is very busy, and unable to do anything about the adjournments."

"Hmm..." How strange that this delay was creating a circumstance that was getting through more on her to-do list than anything else in the last two years. That was unexpected.

"Meg? What is this? You seem distant today."

"I have no idea what you mean." She frowned as she sugared his cup and set it in front of him. Nothing was different from her side, yet his tone was testy. This was a look on Everett Grossman she didn't think was very attractive.

"You know I am very concerned about your well-being since…" He paused and softened his voice. "You know that I care about you. That is why I have not mentioned your repayments. I know you are behind, but you are not to blame for the cattle duffing and all the misfortune that has come your way. If only you would let me help you more. It is not right for a lady to be riding and mustering the way you do. I have men who can do your labouring. This is an ongoing offer that stands."

Meg took a breath and smiled graciously. "Thank you, Everett. You will get your money. And I do appreciate your leniency and your support to keep the repayments manageable. I don't take the loans for granted. But I have to do this with my own resources as much as I can. I need to protect what Alistair and I set up. You know your thoughtfulness has been my lifeline. I have told you this, many times."

"There is the other offer that stands that would solve every aspect of this situation. You still wear your widow's garb, Meg, you don't have to. Think how much more comfortable your life would be at the homestead. And then there would be no debts between us. Most women take twelve months, many less than that. I have tried to be patient and give you space, but I feel you do not respect my feelings by the way you constantly put me off."

There it was again: that unaccountable feeling of pressure. She had received so much kindly support from his quarter that she didn't want to be ungrateful, but just now, she felt cornered. She was not sure how to back out of it politely without alienating the one friend she had through these catastrophic months. She went with the only thing she could think of. She feigned a woman's problem and clutched her abdomen. "Please excuse me, Everett. I feel unwell. I need to attend the bathroom." Closing the door firmly behind her, she fled to the outhouse.

She washed up slowly in the bucket left for that purpose on a stump and took some deep breaths. She was not ready to throw this away. How could she bury Alistair's heart and hard work into another man's estate by marrying him, however sensitive he was to her wellbeing? This was the one thing that kept him alive for her. She still needed this. At some point she would let it go… or it would be taken from her. But not yet. She didn't want to release Alistair just yet. And if it was all to go, she was going to get as much as she could out of it in the process. This might be all she had to keep her future secure. She couldn't be reckless with it, however convenient.

She lingered on the verandah as she heard voices inside. That surprised her. She glanced through the curtained window and saw Everett staring down Ben who was systematically stacking wood in the wood-box. Ben stood up and calmly turned towards him, his tall frame looking at him eye to eye. She opened the door and Everett quickly sat down at the table glaring. Ben went back to stoking the fire. After all his withering remarks, it seemed strange that Everett would be talking with him. She hadn't had one conversation that wasn't work related with the silent man since he arrived. Not really. That hadn't bothered her any. Until now. What could they possibly have to discuss with such energy?

"Would you like to stay for tea, since you have so much to say to our guest?" she said with disparaging sarcasm to her ward with her hand still on the door handle.

"Ain't my guest," said Ben. He stood up and walked around the table to the door waiting for Meg to come inside. He went out and left the door open, sitting on the cane chair out on the verandah.

Meg closed the door firmly and poured her own cup of tea before she sat down. "He doesn't seem like your usual preference for social banter," she observed.

Everett tilted his head. "If it bothers you, it bothers me. Even when it is outside the respectable forms of society, I am not one to stand behind etiquette to just keep up appearances."

Greif! Why had she never noticed that pompous condescension before? How gracious of him to lower his standards so far to bother visiting her! She sipped her tea slowly, trying to think of a response that was not out and out rude.

He took her silence as an invitation to continue. "Meg, you know your unfortunate position means little to me. That's why I'm here: I love you." There. He had made his declaration.

She froze for a moment, and after a while she put down her cup. "Excuse me, Everett, I am going to have to cut our tea short. I have work that requires my attention."

He moved over to her side and put his hand in his pocket. "Meg, surely you cannot leave such a declaration unacknowledged."

"I really do not have the time. My lack of respectable social standing means I don't have the luxury of delegating. There is work to attend to." She stood up and turned away.

"But I said that doesn't matter! After all I have done for you, you must know how I feel. I want to…"

She turned back and cut him off by holding up her hand. "I have no particular investment in your feelings just now, Everett. Only my own," she said.

He pulled his hand out of his pocket and stretched his fingers. "Meg, are you refusing me? You know you cannot survive here alone. You said so yourself. You need me. I need…"

"Please excuse me." She stood tall and the grim line of her mouth went thinner. She stared him down coolly.

He considered her stance and then bowed. He gathered his hat and gloves and walked to the door. "Good afternoon, Mrs McGregor. I trust you will be in a more congenial humour next time I call," he said and went to untether his horse.

She nodded and curtsied. "We'll see," she said through gritted teeth, as he rode off. She spun around and went out to the wood heap. She chopped and split, log after log. She paused and lent on the axe breathing heavily; her eyes squeezed shut. She felt a hand on her wrist. "We have enough wood, Ma'am."

"What if he's right? What if I can't do this by myself?"

"You have up 'til now. Why would that change?"

She opened her eyes and looked at him. "Well that's just it. I feel like I am getting on top of things. Perhaps with you being here, that has helped… but now he's getting all hot and sweaty and demanding."

Ben raised his eyebrows, his expression unreadable.

"What?" It was said spontaneously, without conscious thought.

"It seems Mr Everett Grossman doesn't like his women independent."

"I am not his woman!"

"Huh. Maybe. Still, I reckon he thinks so," he said

with grin. He shrugged. "I'll have that tea now, if it's still on offer." And he gathered up another load of wood and walked back to the house.

6.

Meg did serve tea. She had done so every meal since he arrived, but this time it was different. This time she was conscious that Everett had spoken with him. She was conscious that she had heard their voices in energetic conversation, even if she could not make out their words. She had seen Ben stand up and look him in the eye without fear. It confused her no end.

"Who are you?" she said as she sat down his cup.

"Don't know what you mean, Ma'am."

"Who are you? Where do you come from?"

"Just a Duffer who got caught in the crossfire."

"It wasn't crossfire. I knew exactly where I aimed."

"Okay then. Just a Duffer... who got caught."

"Hmm. I doubt that on a couple of accounts. The main one being that you know Everett. You know him; you used his full name."

"He's a big-wig. Everyone here abouts knows Mr Everett Grossman."

"That's not what I meant. The way you spoke, you are not strangers."

"Well that ain't likely. Me being incarcerated under property-arrest for charges not yet laid. That only happens to no-bodies that people want to lose."

Meg sipped her tea. What had she got herself into

here? "Or does it happen to people they don't want to accuse? All these delays hardly seem like lost paperwork. Who would be working on your account so vigorously?" If that was the case, then she wished that she could have an advocate half so dedicated.

He put down his cup. He had an idea forming in his mind. It had been growing like a tree in an unexpected place and he didn't really know where to start with tending it. He cleared his throat after a while. "Mrs McGregor, I want to move down to the stables. Put me on as your farm-hand."

"What? Why would I do that?" She gasped at the audacity of the notion.

"You need labouring help. You said yourself you are getting on top of things now. I need evidence of good behaviour for my hearing. Not fussed with the idea of a rope around my neck."

"You stole my cattle! I can't afford to pay you even if I was inclined: which I am not. I'm barely making payments. Any other creditor would have taken me to court by now."

"I didn't actually."

"Didn't what?"

"Didn't steel anything."

"You were caught in the act!"

"But I have no cattle in my possession."

"Well no. Neither do I. Because... you aided and abetted the someone who does! The only reason you don't have them is because I stopped you. You're nuts if you think any judge will look benevolently on your position. But perhaps that is a gamble you are willing to take."

"I know the risks. I need to mitigate them. That's why I need to work for you. You pay me wages and I'll pay board and keep; what's left can go towards paying off what the lost stock would have brought at the sale... fair market price. You'll not be out of pocket, and I get what I need to improve my chances with the Magistrate."

"You are actually serious! How can you conceivably think I will ever consider what you propose?"

He shrugged. "Where else are you going to get the labouring you need, to stay on top of this?"

"You could run."

He nodded. "I can. But I haven't."

The truth of that suddenly hit her. She spun around and stared at him. "Why? Why haven't you made a run for it?" she said hoarsely. Again, she almost wished he would so she wouldn't have to be bothered with him.

"Because this is my best chance. The charges are not yet firm. However, being a fugitive from the Law: that's a bullet or a noose for sure. I think I just like living."

"You're counting on me dropping the charges!"

He grinned. "Ain't putting my eggs in that basket. I'm okay with poor odds, but I'm not an idiot."

"Well, as long as you understand that is never going to happen. You leave here for one reason only: to face the Magistrate."

He raised his eyebrows, almost as if he was daring her to remain firm in her resolve. But he said nothing. He was amused by the idea that this effectively made him her bond-slave. Stay, work, live. Leave, and be pursued by the Law until he was killed. Even he didn't consider that left him with much of a choice.

That evening after tea when the night chores were done, he didn't come inside to bunk down on his swag. Meg went out to the verandah and he was sitting on the cane settee, looking at the stars. He leant forward his arms resting comfortably on his knees. "Ma'am I would really like you to consider my proposition."

"I have considered it. I am not going to employ someone who stole my cattle. I can't trust you. You could be planning on systematically stripping my entire place. As soon as the Doctor gives you clearance and the Constable comes and gets you… you are gone."

He sighed and sat back. Settled. He returned to looking at the stars.

"Come inside now. I need to go to bed."

"Goodnight then."

Meg frowned slightly. He didn't move. She wondered then if that meant he would be gone in the morning. If that were his choice, it would be a relief. "Oh.

Well. Goodnight."

In the morning, as Meg came out from the bedroom, she quickly glanced at the swag. It remained undisturbed. She opened the front door, and Ben was slumped across the settee, asleep. "Oh. You're still here." An unaccountable feeling sitting in the middle of her chest surprised her. She covered a smile. "Get some wood and light the fire while I sort breakfast. We're going to bring the calves in today for marking."

He opened his eyes without moving. "I ain't your farmhand."

"No, but you can contribute while you are here. You eat my food and sleep in my house."

"Didn't last night. Happy to sort my own grub too. I know the constable has given you rations for me being here."

"Oh!" And she stormed off to the outhouse, and he quietly watched her go with an amused glint in his eye. She brought some firewood back on her way and stomped loudly passed him, knocking his boot, without apology, that hung out over the arm of the chair, as she opened the door. She knew it to be his weak ankle. She cooked her breakfast and made a particular effort to make sure it smelt amazing. She dressed in her mustering gear and when she looked in the mirror she tucked a stray hair in behind her ear. She reined her horse in close to the verandah-rail, on her way out the paddocks. "I'm going out now. Should be back about lunchtime," she said.

He lay on the settee, hat down over his eyes. He barely moved and acknowledged her with a wave of his hand. She impatiently dug her heels in and cantered out through the gate. How perplexing! Perhaps he had decided to go. Or perhaps he had made up his mind to sit this out. Well she had done 'alone' for eighteen months. She could do another day's work by herself. Besides he would get restless. He didn't do 'nothing' easily. She knew that much about him and she could lay a solid bet that by tomorrow he would relent purely out of boredom. Not that it mattered to her one way or the other. Marking calves was definitely a two-man job though. She could carry that over. She would have to.

He lay on that settee until she rode out to the paddocks. When she was gone, he drove himself hard through an exercise routine: push-ups and pull-ups and sit-ups. He ran down to the creek and swam across the waterhole a number of times. He found his knife where Meg had put it in the cupboard and practiced throwing it with either hand, using his injured arm. He returned the knife to its possie, and by the time Meg came riding into the yards, he was back on the settee, tired, dozing off.

She looked around convinced she would see evidence of work that he had done while she was out. But the axe stayed embedded in the same stump; the wood box stayed empty; the horses remained stabled. Nothing? That was strange. Any time she tried to enlist him to do something, he simply replied, "I ain't your farmhand. Put me on the books; I'm more than willing to pitch-in."

After a few days of this routine, Ben felt his accuracy rebuilding. And Meg's anger was beyond bounds. Perhaps he was right. Perhaps they had forgotten him, and he was here to be lost. Perhaps she hadn't wanted to admit that she felt safe with him camping in her living room. That evening she rolled up his swag and dumped it at his feet. She served two plates of stew, brought them out to the verandah and plonked one in his lap. "I don't want you camping on my front porch like a mangy stray dog. You can move into the shed."

"And...?"

"And what?"

"This would mean you are putting me on?"

"Well... yes, you can help out some."

"Like you're doing me a favour. I want it in writing. That you are employing me; what you are paying me; what is to be taken off for lodging and food... and don't forget the cattle tab."

"Really, is that necessary?"

"I need the documents for court. Otherwise it means squat. Any more accusations of me taking advantage would not look good. My intention is to buffer the allegation I've got over my head, not add to it."

"Allegation? I caught you! Why does this detail seem

to constantly escape your notice? Besides, I really didn't expect you to be one who was worried about looking good. Come in, and I'll write what you need. Early start. I want to be marking and branding tomorrow. No clean-skins in this herd. You can tell your friends that."

"Ain't my friends," he said, as he followed her inside.

Meg woke to the sound of wood chopping. He came in and filled the wood-box, lit the fire, and put the kettle on to boil. She threw a shawl around her shoulders and came out.

"Morning Ma'am," he said, as he grabbed the chook bucket and the milk bucket for the house cow.

"Ben?"

"Yes Ma'am?"

She hardly knew what she wanted to say. She turned away and said, "Breakfast in half an hour."

"I won't be holding you up any Ma'am."

They worked until late like a well-oiled machine; cogs meshing together in synchronised rhythm. Afterwards, they sat at the table, weary and pleased at what they had got through. He absently rubbed his shoulder as they talked about what had gone well, and addressed what needed attention on the morrow.

Ben screened off the back of the stables from the workshop area as his quarters and made himself a bunk and a table. It wasn't what he would call comfortable, but it served a purpose. He had marked out a space that was his own.

Progressively the shed was sorted so that they could make use of Alistair's tools, which had sat idle for the most part of two years. Ben worked hard, deferring to Meg's plans and good sense. They averted a calving disaster and sorted water issues. They check the boundary fences and reinforced the yards with a more secure gating system. Ben was able to advise first hand where those weaknesses lay. The house surrounds were tidied. He mended the plough; tilled and planted a section for some corn, potatoes and pumpkins. They sweated and laughed and haggled their way through.

By the end of the next week, Meg had regained the momentum that had stalled. By the end of the fortnight, there was a light in her eyes and confidence in her step. Just on the month, she was talking projected plans to clear away her debts. Hope had peeked its head above the horizon.

One night after dinner, Meg sat with her account books and pen and together they were going through the progress they were making. As she finished her calculations, she found they had enough this month to cover her bills and repayments, with a little left over. In that jubilant moment of victory, she turned towards Ben laughing and kissed him square on the mouth. Instantly he responded, caught in that moment; they lingered there, as natural as birdsong at dawn.

Suddenly she opened her eyes, as if she realised where she was. She froze. Ben stopped and dropped his hands, and sat back in his chair. He glanced her way, but didn't say anything, waiting for the tirade to come. He knew it would. What he didn't expect was the look of loathing that came into Meg's eyes. Would his past ever be reconciled? Of all his regrets, this was the one he measured as the greatest. She pushed her chair back and retreated, not behind work or position or responsibility, but behind another wall too high for him to scale.

He stood to his feet. "I'm going back to the stables now Ma'am. Goodnight." And he turned and made himself walk resolutely out the door.

He sat on his bunk for a long time. The farm cat jumped up on his lap and he scratched her back in a companionable sort of way as it purred its guttural rumble. Meg had kissed him. She did that. In a forgotten moment, she reached out. Spontaneously. Naturally. Exuberantly. Irresistibly. Sleep escaped him, and he wondered how he could reassure her that he would never take advantage. He wished in a way there had been a rant. It was easier, more predictable, and left no doubt as to what she was thinking. A blustery squall that was short-lived and then over. This? He didn't know this distant, taciturn, confused silence. He wasn't familiar with that.

Eventually he got up and sat outside in an old chair,

leaning back against the shed wall and watched the stars. Wisps of cloud floated over the thin slither of a moon. A lone cow bellowed, a low, mournful, distant sound in the night. He looked towards the house and watched the lamplight still shining yellow in the window, the curtains blowing a grey sort of shadow across it, as they moved in the night breeze. He saw her stand in the doorway with a lantern. He wondered, as she stepped down from the verandah, if she was going to seek him out. When she got to the holding yards she turned and tracked up over to the hill. He knew it to be the hill where Alistair was buried.

Ben followed as she stumbled towards those little white pickets that bordered the Petrea graves. Alistair's headstone stood beside a nameless grave, and some other markers of those who, over the years, had succumbed to mortality. He stayed in the dark outside the small rim of yellow light cast by the lantern. He was there, not to say anything. Not to do anything. Just to be a guardian standing sentry, in case things got out of hand. He told himself that he didn't need her doing anything desperate. If she was to harm herself in her guilt or grief, there was a reality for him that would not "look good". She was right: looking good had never been a priority for him before. He understood now why it had become absolutely necessary.

She opened the little gate and knelt down, starting to yank the weeds away from the stone border in the shards of light from the lantern. She pushed through the pain in her fingers and tugged relentlessly on the burrs and tough prickles. She gasped for breath, not at the bleeding cuts or the grazes on her knuckles, but at the pain in her chest, reprimanding herself again and again for her neglect. She leant her cheek against the cold stone that bore his name and spoke through her tears to one who had understood her so completely.

No one had ever told her that this unyielding agony would go on and on. No one had ever told her what it would take to survive everyone's good advice. Move on. Marry. Sell out. No one ever asked what she wanted. Yet she had persisted and stayed. But for a moment she had forgotten; and the guilt of that feather-light freedom was worse than the dark mire of pain she was so familiar with. She wanted him back. She wanted the nightmare to be over. She wanted him so much to hold her and tell her what to do, where to look. In a world where she had believed hard work and determination could achieve just about anything, she could not understand why Alistair would always be out of reach.

7.

As the night sky started to fade and a tinge of pink washed across the bank of dull clouds that outlined the mountains, it started to drizzle rain. Meg lay on the mound that bore her husband's body. The cold seeping into her bones felt like the death that gripped him. Nearly two years! Two years and the pain was still as raw as in the beginning. Raw like someone had taken to her body with a cat-of-nine-tails and had not stopped at forty lashes minus one.

As the miserable grey dawn light began to define her motionless form, Ben edged closer. He didn't want to intrude, but this was too long. He leant over her, wet muddy hair clinging to her face, her lips blue-grey from cold. Her cheeks and forehead streaked with grime; mud and blood from her ragged fingers smeared over her clothes. She did not move when he pressed her shoulder; a groan escaped from the back of her throat.

He picked her up and carried her back to the house. She laid shivering on the bed and he removed her wet clothes and boots. He covered her clean petticoat with the quilt and tucked it in firm. He stoked the fire and put the water on to boil. He filled a hot water bladder and wrapped it in a towel and placed it near her cold feet. He took the naked, skinned rabbit hanging in the meat safe and put it on for stew and broth. He wiped her face clean, with a warm cloth and washed her hands in the basin, and applied a salve to the cuts. He didn't want anyone coming here and seeing her looking like they had had a brawl. He covered her shoulders with a clean shawl. She was exhausted and slept through most of it.

Ben attended to the chores, always checking in. He even mopped the mud from the floor out of boredom. He came in after chopping more wood in the rain and found her struggling out of bed to go to the bathroom. He carried her there, and back, water clinging to her frame. He poured more water for her ablutions behind the screen and with averted eyes handed her a clean dry nightgown. The pure intimacy of these tasks, mundane and ordinary, had his head spinning. In every way, a kiss was easier to dismiss. He remembered how Meg had nursed him back from death; she had been so vocal about how that had been distasteful for her. In contrast this was an agreeable duty. In that moment he could not think of anything he wouldn't do to see her well and feisty once more.

She slept all day. And as she slept on, soothed by the sound of rain on the shingles, the tension in his mind began to build to explosion point. He had chopped all the wood he could, so he dug a section of a garden bed near the house, turning the sodden clods with a shovel. He added mulch from the stables and turned it again. He dug a couple of holes where Meg had thought some shade trees would be of benefit, and so he transplanted wild saplings there. Just one of those many things she and Alistair had spoken about, but never got to. Like the house-yard fence Meg had once mentioned in passing. A fence sounded like a project. Close to the house. He marked out the string-line and post-holes... and started digging, rain dripping from the brim of his hat. He was desperate to dissipate the pressure that was building like a volcano in his body. He went down to the shed and brought back his swag and set it up in the corner. When she stirred, he poured some strained broth into a pannikin and held it for her as her hands trembled with exhaustion. She lay back against the pillows and slept until morning.

The next day he did the same. After her breakfast she sat up in bed looking blankly out the window at the rain sodden landscape. It was then she noticed the string-line and post-holes marking out her fence. She was bed-ridden; there was no one to call him to account. He didn't have to do this or any other thing. He came in to collect her dishes. "Why? Why do you work so hard? Why don't you hate me?" Her eyes flashed with her desperate question.

His brow clouded. Could she not see? He could only assume such blindness was based on her own deep-seated loathing. What is hated must surely hate in return. He couldn't deny she had her reasons. If she wouldn't hear the messages of remorse from his hard work, his patient unchallenged support; the persistent effort to make restitution, then words would certainly not be heard either.

Instead he offered something else. "I met your husband once…"

Instantly Meg's eyes turned to face him. "You did? You knew him?"

"No, I didn't know him. We just met. Casually. He was flooded in. Couldn't get back home so he stayed at the pub overnight. We shared a pint. But I remember the way he spoke. I had never heard a man speak with such respect the way Alistair McGregor did that night. He said something that always stuck with me…"

Meg shook her head, wading through the fog of malaise. "I'm sorry… you met Alistair? He spoke of me… us… and you… you targeted us for duffing?"

"No! I had no idea. That was just after I came to Farthing. I didn't even connect that conversation until I'd been here a while. They never told me whose place it was going to be. I'd probably do different now."

"Probably? That's the best you can do? Probably?" She was disgusted. She tried to get out of bed, but doubled over in a fit of coughing, and then lying back propped up by pillows. She was unable to move from fatigue that gripped her body and pinned her to the covers.

He looked suspiciously at the flush in her cheeks, her eyes wild. He felt the back of her hand, and then her forehead. This fire in her eyes wasn't just indignation, she was burning with fever. He wet some cloths and wiped the perspiration around her face and neck. He went to the cabinet and took one of the tinctures marked "Febrile Sweats" that the doctor had left, whether for Alistair or himself, he was unsure. He dispensed it and Meg sipped and scowled, and dozed off soon after.

For days he stayed close. Every so often Meg struggled to sit up, groaning with fatigue, coughing and she'd mumble about going out to check the cattle. He reassured her it was all taken care of, and she reluctantly surrendered to more sleep.

Early on the ninth morning she came out of the bedroom and looked at him lying on the swag in the corner. "Oh. You're back in my house. Does that mean you've resigned as my farmhand?"

He blinked hard as he forced his eyes open and propped his arm under his head. He relaxed a little as he looked at her eyes, circled with dark rings, but clear from fever. "No Ma'am. Different duties that's all. I'll be going back to the shed as soon as you're okay."

"Well I'm okay," she said. She felt pathetically weak, but at least she could get out of bed.

His head thumped, every muscle complained, and his shoulder ached mercilessly. He had pushed himself ruthlessly, and suddenly it felt like a train had hit him head on. "Oh, I guess I'll go then." He didn't move for a while, and then he sat up slowly.

"Ben?" He turned as he was pulling his shirt on. "I know what you did. I don't know how long it's been, but..."

"About four days Ma'am."

"Oh. That long? It was a bad fever then."

"Believe you did the same for me a while back."

"Well, I am pretty sure I resented saving your life. I've been lying here thinking. I don't remember much, but I know that you were here, and well, that is appreciated. I am genuinely grateful I wasn't alone."

He nodded. "I'll be going back to the stables then Ma'am." He paused. "And I'm taking a couple of days off. I'm bushed."

"I think that is fair." He stood up and started to gather his things. "Ben?"

"Hmm?"

"What did Alistair say to you that night at the pub? He didn't drink, and he was not a man given to lose talk."

He blinked again, his head cloudy from exhaustion. "Oh. I thought you wouldn't remember... from the fever."

"I was sick, but it didn't fry my brain."

He frowned thoughtfully. Feisty was back. That was good, but the way she had reacted he was not so sure that she would want to hear the conversation between them. "I bought him a drink, but he never finished it, so he certainly wasn't drunk. We were just sitting there having a chat and then he had some sort of attack. He was in a lot of pain, so I helped him up to his room. He said being together didn't mean giving up being the hero of their story. He encouraged me to do the same if I ever got a chance to meet a girl like his Meg... she was smart, capable, beautiful... and could shoot like a deadeye. He said I could still tackle wild brumbies, walk on live coals, climb uncharted mountains: whatever it is that I do. To use my 'strong'... for her. Use it to keep her safe. Since being here I've thought about that... to be more; more than just tough, or maybe more than I was. Anyway, he said he'd sleep it off and be okay, but I went and got Doc Mansfield anyway. Before I left, he said that we all have our fights and reasons to keep fighting. You kept him fighting. He was fighting for his Meg."

"Oh. *'His Meg'*..." Her eyes softened and there was the gentle glisten of a tear.

He turned away and allowed her moment of remembering. He went to the water pitcher to pour himself a drink, and he paused with the glass in his hand. "I'm known for being reckless, but I didn't worry too much about taming my ways because, after that conversation, I figured I would never meet any person worthy of that sort of fight. My brother has someone like that; Alistair did too, but well, I was none too convinced I would meet such a girl. I wasn't in a good place so I reckoned it didn't matter anyway. I figured I had nothing much left to aim for."

"And now?"

"Now? Oh, Meg, if you knew how many mountains I have climbed these last months!"

"Oh…"

"Just so you know. I would climb more…" His voice cracked from fatigue and he cleared his throat to cover his embarrassment. It sounded like he was choked with emotion. "I will…" The thought got lost and he wished he could have this conversation when his head was clearer. The effect on Meg was entirely beguiling.

"I don't think I cried when he died. There was too much going on. I never did that."

He stood there watching her. Numb and uncertain. She was peaking her head back around that wall, and he didn't want to startle her. "Well… if you need to… again… you know, need to go back there… we could plant a garden maybe. Like a proper one. But not in the rain…" It sounded dumb. He shrugged. He didn't know what else to say.

She looked at him curiously. "I would like that. I wouldn't have thought you'd consider that important."

What he thought was important didn't matter just now. "He taught me about respect in a way no boss ever did. Perhaps this is a way of giving it back."

"I like Zinnias. They are tough. He was like that."

He had no idea what a zinnia was but nodded anyway. He turned to roll up his swag, when they heard a couple of visitors ride up to the house. Meg went to the door, coughing into her handkerchief. Grossman and Constable Matthews were dismounting.

Matthews tipped his hat. "Morning Mrs McGregor. I've come to bring in the prisoner. The charges need to be finalised so that we can catch the next court sitting."

"I'm dropping them."

Matthews blinked. "I'm sorry? What?"

"I'm not pressing charges."

"You can't do that.

"I can and I have. I will write out whatever is needed to that effect."

"But you have been requesting my attention to this matter for a while now."

"Exactly. And it fell on deaf ears."

Grossman frowned. "Cattle thieving is a criminal act defying the law and order of our land."

"It was nigh four months ago. Has any progress been made on finding the other offender?"

Matthews shifted his feet, looked vague and shook his head.

"I want him taken him away and charged," Grossman fumed. "He'll be after my stock next."

"If he was planning to rampage across the region, I dare say he would have done it by now. There has been plenty of opportunity. This wasn't a crime against you."

"We came all this way. I want this felon facing court!" Grossman blustered.

"Fascinating that you consider yourself so inconvenienced. This hasn't been a bother for the duration of his time here. Why is it now suddenly urgent?"

Grossman scowled. "I approached the court dozens of times on your behalf. Meg, I was advocating for your case."

"Were you now? Doesn't say much for your influence then does it?"

Matthews heard Grossman growl and quickly cleared his throat and stepped forward. "The back-log has cleared. He is ready for processing now."

"I'm letting you know we made a private out-of-court settlement of restitution, which has been fully complied with. You couldn't be moved when I wanted you to, so I managed the situation according to my personal satisfaction. I'm sorry, but this no longer is a matter I am pursuing."

Matthews quickly justified the delays since local resources had been drawn into dealing with the spat of stagecoach robberies. He stated emphatically that these crimes had been dealt with appropriately and his obligations were now to follow up on her report in a timely manner.

"Timely?" Meg hesitated. What he was saying didn't make sense. Perhaps she was still feverish and not thinking clearly. She wanted to find out what was behind the bizarre handling of this matter. "There was also the problem of evidence. Constable Matthews, you told me that I didn't have much of a case. You were very firm on the point of unsubstantiated claims. What has changed?"

"We can estimate your herd, and the number stolen.

It will be all taken into account, so that the full measure of the law will be applied," he said formally.

Meg stared at him. "There is no need to estimate. I gave you accurate numbers right at the beginning."

"Oh right. Yes. And I have those details in my reports. We wish to see justice done to your case, Ma'am."

"I have no intention of handing him over. Like I said, he has provided restitution in a suitably remorseful manner."

Grossman started to protest again, and Matthews held up his hand. "Would you mind showing me, Ma'am, the terms of this agreement?" Meg saw him give Grossman a sideways look with a nod and a smirk. Grossman calmed immediately with a dark smile hovering around his eyes.

Meg felt a prickle up her spine. Ben came and stood by her side. "Just show them the paper."

"This is rubbish. There is no justice here!"

"Never said there was. Just show them the paper."

Grossman's voice became a quiet hiss. "Perhaps it is not just remorse that has turned your head, Mrs McGregor. Your husband would roll in his grave at what's going on under his roof."

"You leave Alistair out of this! You have no idea what's going on under my roof!" She turned on her heel and came out with the ledger. "I have been ill and the last few days are not up to date. My projections expect him to be cleared of any responsibility come the end of the month."

She paused for a moment and continued, "But then, while I was unwell, he took on extra responsibilities, longer hours… which rightly should be paid at a higher rate. So perhaps he is out of debt already."

Matthews looked at the book with a raised brow turning a couple of pages back. He returned the book to her hand. "Last fortnight aside, it does seem to be in order," he reluctantly acknowledged. Matthews handed her a card to say they had been calling and requested that she give them a statement within the week confirming that no further investigation was required.

"I'll do that now. There is no point in drawing this out." Matthews dated and witnessed her statements. She handed Ben a copy and passed the other one to Matthews. He nodded and avoided looking at Grossman.

"Mrs McGregor, you would do well to attend to your other matters with the same diligence," Grossman observed grimly as they walked to the door.

"Meaning?"

"Meaning, that if you can pay a workman, you can pay outstanding accounts."

"Are you threatening me?"

"Obviously to do so with a law-man by my side would be foolishness."

"Well, the Law-man has my statement. Right now, you need to leave. Good day gentlemen."

Meg watched them stiffly mount and ride away. Her

frame trembled as she melted on the step, her energy sapped. Ben had not moved. Slowly he walked down the steps carrying his swag. "I'm going to my quarters now Ma'am."

"Ben. Stay. Please stay."

"They are gone now. They won't be back soon."

She couldn't account for that uncanny sense of dread. "Just stay... use my bed to sleep. You are exhausted."

He smiled... tired. "Only one way I'm ever going to sleep in your bed, Meg... and this ain't it."

8.

She walked back inside and latched the door behind her. It didn't seem possible that in the space of a week she could go from feeling like they were on top of a working plan, to again wading through quicksand, sucking her down, physically and emotionally spent. She lay down and closed her eyes, but that gloating sneer of Grossman kept taunting her rest. She turned over and squeezed her eyes tight and willed herself to think of something from a safer time, not related to now, but it was not Alistair that turned to face her. It was the imprint of Ben's frame that stayed with her: bent over tending the fire; passing her a drink; digging post-holes and setting rails outside her window, rain dripping off the brim of his hat; bringing her soup; changing her sweat drenched sheets.

She slept until early afternoon and the relief of further sleep escaped her so she got up and made stew for dinner. She did the daily chores before tackling some baking with fresh eggs from the chook yard. Everywhere she looked she saw something else that Ben had started or completed during her confinement of bed-ridden fever. She shook her head. Why? He never did answer that feverish question. All of this effort was over and above, and it defied her conclusions. Climbing mountains, he had said. If she didn't know better, she would think that this had the look of walking on live coals for her. Eventually, she lay down again, drained and depleted, and she slept fitfully through the night.

She rose late, and, after the chores, she addressed the accounts and the ledger. She looked at the numbers and put down the pen. She sat with a particular thought for a long time. She realised that regardless of the tally at the bottom of the page, there was no debt left. In her heart, the debt was cleared. It occurred to her, as she sat there, that this had been over a while ago, and she wondered why she had kept the ledger going: pedantically keeping tally on a debt that no longer existed. Her brow gathered in a frown and she pursed her lips as she realised that she was keeping him here under obligation, and now that was no longer acceptable. She had to let him go. She picked up the quill and released him with a stroke of her pen. It surprised her that as she folded the paper, how it felt like walking into a dark, disused room with a faint flickering candle. And with the blurry dim light there came another feeling: a realisation that she had no idea of what was in this room. It was unfamiliar, yet intriguing, and there was an irresistible desire to become acquainted and comfortable here, to spring-clean the corners and the rugs and to shine the furniture, so that it would become a room to be shared.

Later that afternoon, she took the basket from the kitchen table and went down to the stables. She opened the large door and stepped into the shadows. She had never been behind those screens in the back corner and it seemed to her that she was trespassing on very private ground. But that driving curiosity to see the personal life of Ben Harker had not abated... to tread there and be part of it. It was strange that even during his imposed incarceration he never held himself like an underling; he always contributed to their deliberations energetically, as an equal, with initiative and logic. But he never talked about himself, his past, what he liked, or what he wanted for the future.

She stood beside the screen and realised there was nowhere to knock on these hessian dividers. After a while she edged around them quietly. Ben was asleep on his bunk. There was a small trestle table where she put down the basket. She looked around. These quarters were Spartan to say the least. His jacket and hat hung on a bearer that had been decked with a few metal pegs. There was an array of shelves made out of wooden packing boxes that held some of Alistair's old shirts and socks that she had handed over to get him through. There were a couple of other items: a small, yellowed photo creased from wear... and a few books he had borrowed from her shelf. Another packing case became his wash-stand with a chipped enamel basin that looked like it had been salvaged from the dump.

Ben opened his eyes and put his arm under his head. He watched her silently as she surveyed his ordered, meagre life. He lay there, wondering at this visit. She had never ventured in here before.

Rather than despising its lack, Meg considered the cause of it. A reckless, capable, hardworking man, not given to drink, would normally have more to show for it. What was his story? She was curiously touched by this display of his personal world and speculated about his family. Where were they? She picked up the tattered photo and realised this was a wedding portrait. Oh, my goodness! His wedding portrait! He stood tall beside his bride, proud and pleased. He was married! She put it back as if it was hot and it fell to the floor. She hurriedly picked it up and propped it against the timber shelf and smoothed her hands on her skirt. Saved from a big mistake! She adjusted it, so it looked like it had not been moved.

Ben quickly closed his eyes feigning sleep. She turned to check he was undisturbed, and went over to the basket, disappointment tugging at her throat. Guess that explained the silence. Ben yawned and stretched and opened his eyes. She heard him stir, put on a smile and turned. He noticed immediately remoteness in her manner.

"I'm sorry to wake you but I didn't want you to have to worry about coming up to the house. I brought you some stew, and I did some baking..."

"Baking? That's new."

"No, not really. I do that sometimes when I am thinking about things. That visit from Grossman disturbed me some."

"Happy to be the recipient of your remedial activities

then."

"Well, I'll leave you to it. Thank you again for helping me…"

"Meg?" She paused at the screens. "Would you stay and eat dinner with me?"

"Why?"

"Well, you've never been here before. Seems like the hospitable thing to do."

"I don't know Ben…"

"It's just food. We have eaten with our feet under the same table before." He sat up on his bunk and reached for his shirt and pulled it on.

The scars were raised and red as he rolled his shoulder and stretched. She looked away, uncomfortable. His presence never affected her when she nursed him on her living room floor, wounded and vulnerable, when his pain had almost been a joy. What about when they were mustering or branding —when his reckless skill was tough and efficient, and meant survival for her? But now it did? Why now, when she discovered he was unavailable? No longer an option. Thank goodness she had found out. She would regulate her manner accordingly: business as usual.

"Well, okay then. I do have to eat," she said efficiently. Nothing has to change. Keep to practical.

He grabbed a couple of wooden packing boxes and pulled them up to the table. He covered one with a shirt to avoid the rough timber snagging her skirts and offered it to her as if it was a fine upholstered, carved-back dining chair. He pulled the plates from the basket and supressed a smile. She had brought down *two* table-settings. He handed her the cutlery and served the meal.

She nodded and sat, and wished she wasn't blushing. It seemed she had nothing to say, and eating filled in the gaps. But although he appeared relaxed enough with her there in his territory, he said nothing. She felt obliged to try some sort of conversation. "So... umm... it doesn't look that comfortable here. I should have checked before this to see if you needed anything. I apologise. Not a very thoughtful employer."

"It does okay. Only sleep here anyway. And it gives me space to think if I need to." He smiled at her. "I didn't arrive with much," he said.

"Ahh. No. That is true." Why would he remind her of those dreadful circumstances that caused him to be here? She wanted to blank that out.

"So, the thing that I noticed about the visit from Matthews and Grossman, was that you took it upon yourself to do something that you said you would never do. I found that an interesting turn on your resolve."

"Everything I said was true. I wasn't going to just hand you over, when justice was the furthest thing from their mind. I would like to know what is going on."

"Those guys keep their own counsel. Didn't expect Matthews to be in Grossman's pocket though. That was a surprise."

"I caught up on the bookwork this morning and I've completed the ledger. It was hardly just four days I was unwell. It was nigh on a fortnight if I am to believe the date on Matthews' card. However, it does mean I was right. Your tally is done. You have fulfilled your obligations here. There is no more debt." She pulled a folded sheet from the basket and handed it to him.

He read it and put it to the side. "So, what now?"

"I don't know. I promised I won't be placing any charges against you. I stand by that."

"So, I stole your cattle. You shot me. Instead of letting me die, you saved my life. Instead of incarcerating me, you allowed me to work off the debt. I have restored what was taken and I nursed you when you were ill. Sounds like we are square."

"Sounds like it."

"No reason to stay."

"Sounds like it."

"But I was hoping to stay on. Like it here."

"I've been trying to think of a way. I thought I had a plan, but that seems to have come to naught. I can't pay you. You know I would if I could."

"So, what was the plan you had to abandon?"

She smiled. Honest banter was good. She liked that about how they were with each other. And she wanted to shock him. "I was going to ask you to marry me."

He laughed. "Going to. Changed your mind when you saw my lack of earthly goods and zero accumulated wealth?"

"Oh yes. That was a significant part of my reckoning."

"Well. I guess it is good you found out before you got in too deep then."

She looked at him square in the eyes. "It was definitely good I found out before I got in too deep."

He smiled again, relaxed and unperturbed. "Oh. The photograph."

"Yes, the photograph!"

"What about it?" As if he didn't know!

"Well, the woman in the photograph... is she still alive?"

"Believe so. Had a couple of kids last time I saw her."

"Don't you think it is kind of important to know that the man I love is married with a family and I was about to..." It was out before she realised. This time she did blush. She stood up and turned away. Oh, this would never do!

Her confession didn't astonish him. It was more her look of horror that had him wondering. "Well, they ain't my kids."

"As if that makes it more acceptable!" Her mind spun with this undeclared history. "And yet, you keep the photograph? You love her still? Grief! This is messy."

He shrugged. "Love her? Not really. Ain't my photograph."

"Of course, it's your photograph. You are standing there with her!"

"Well, yes, the photograph is mine… but it ain't my wedding. Ain't my bride."

"It looks very much like you!"

"It does, yes."

"Who is she then? Is she your sister?"

"Ain't my sister… sister-in-law. That's my brother. His wedding."

She turned and looked at him and scoffed. "You seriously expect me to swallow that? You carry around a photograph of your brother's wedding? That is ridiculous. Who does that?"

He shrugged. "I got a niece and a nephew. Good looking little tykes. Take after their Uncle Ben."

"That's your brother?"

"We look alike. Not exactly identical, but close enough. He has bigger ears. We'd stand in front of the mirror as kids and work it out. And we did the usual swapping over and afterwards think the people we tricked were really stupid. To us it was obvious. That photograph served me well, mostly to keep clingy girls away. But here… here it was a reminder of family and what that was like. I hadn't wanted to remember that until I came here."

"Oh." That was quite a speech. It was the first time

he had spoken of his family. Or himself. Or of anything much.

"Does that help?" he asked.

"Help with what?"

"The abandoned plan..."

"Oh." She turned around, her heart beating. She was trying not to look flustered. She sat back down again. "Well, I guess. It could be a possibility I suppose."

"What do you need to make it a certainty?"

"Oh. Umm. I'm not sure..."

He laughed again. "I feel like I'm applying for a job. Do you need information? What?"

"No. I just need to know you love me!" She snapped at him.

"There's more to it than that. You know I love you. You do, Meg. You would never have changed your mind about me if you weren't sure of that. So, there is something else."

"Perhaps... Oh grief! I want a drink. Would you come up to the house? Please?" She stacked the plates self-consciously.

"Okay then." He picked up the basket and walked with her to the door. The sun was bleeding over the horizon and he paused a moment to look at it. "Meg. Whatever it is... we'll work it out. We'll find a way... the payments to Grossman... all of that."

She nodded and walked on in silence. Eventually she

pointed to the cattle-yards, "This was Alistair's dream."

"I thought it was your dream."

"Well… yes, but not so much. It was his mostly. I was… caretaking for him really."

"So how long does that go on then? You know… now that he is… well, up on the hill."

"See. I don't know. I thought forever…" Her voice faded and cracked. She was looking at a monster that she had never wanted to acknowledge inhabited her wardrobe.

Ben frowned but said nothing. How could he be the caretaker of another man's dream? He wasn't sure how that worked. He wasn't here for Alistair McGregor.

Meg stumbled on a loose stone in the fading light and he instinctively he dropped the basket and reached out to catch her. She stayed in his arms for a time. Eventually she turned her face to his and kissed him. He was watching her closely. The last time she kissed him, she ran. But almost as if she was testing the water, she closed her eyes and kissed him again. Eventually she pulled away.

"Did I pass?" he asked softly.

"What do you mean?"

"It seems like that was more of the job interview."

"Last time… I panicked. I wondered if I could do it again."

"Well, seems only right we should check that again then." He stepped forward and pulled her in. As they released their embrace, he smiled down at her. "So? No bolting?"

"No. It seems not."

"Well we've clarified a couple of things. I'm not married. I potentially will have good-looking kids. I love you. I kiss okay. What's next?"

"You are making fun of me."

"Actually, you invited me for a drink. This is the slowest walk to the house on record."

She chuckled a confession and stepped up the pace. She paused on the verandah, before opening the door. "Ben… this is unfamiliar territory for me."

"Me too," he said with a smile. He stood there with an unaccountable sense of coming home. As Meg lit the lamp in the evening shadows, he looked around with the realisation of what this could be and what it might mean. It was still an unfamiliar, uneasy thought. He sat down on the lounge and she poured that drink from the cabinet. They had never shared a drink like this before.

"Don't you have any ambitions of your own?" she asked eventually.

"Sure. But it seems they are changing."

"What do you mean?"

"Sometimes we are given a chance to support the dreams of another and, in the process, find our own fulfilled. You had that. Maybe it's my turn."

"Hmm. Philosopher."

He grinned. "There may be more to Ben Harker than

cattle duffing."

"You like it that you have this colourful history of criminal activity!" she accused.

"I like it that I got rescued. I don't ever want to forget that."

She frowned. "Oh..."

"What?"

"I just... well, I never thought I rescued you. You were helping me. You were saving me. You were walking on live coals for me."

"Still am. Meg, you must know... I'm not here to care-take another man's dream. I am only here for you. So, if this ain't it, that's okay."

"But I don't do anything else. This is it. This is all I know."

"That's fine. As long as it is yours. Be certain it's your dream."

"Well. What if it's not this? What do I do then?" She stood up and restlessly arranged the kettle on the stove.

"You sell it. Shouldn't be too hard to find a buyer. Grossman's been all over you for it. Although I think he was hoping to get it for free, or at least for the price of a fairly ordinary betrothal-ring."

Her frown deepened. "I don't want to sell. Not now. You being here, that's changed things. But..." There was an unarticulated reservation that was bothering her.

"But?" He tracked her movements around the

kitchen recess until she finally sat down in a lounge chair opposite him.

"As a widow I have property and income... and yes, debts. But they are mine. As a wife, I have nothing."

"Ah. Marrying me will be a backward step."

"Marrying anyone would be a backward step... in that way."

"There may be ways to settle that... legally."

"It's the legal things I have no head for."

"Where's your will kept then?"

"Mine? I don't have one."

"You don't?"

"Alistair left Petrea Downs to me. He was very definite about it. It was to be kept in trust for... our... our son. But..." She paused and said nothing for a long time. She retreated into the shadows of the chair and a deep haunted look traced the lines of her face. Ben went over to her in the dim light of the lamp and knelt down in front of her. She gasped and a sob escaped her diaphragm as she reached out and clung to him.

"Meg? You and Alistair had a kid?"

"They said it was impossible... but the impossible happened. I was about six months on when Alistair..." Her voice faded out. "With everything going on I went into labour early. Everyone had left after the funeral."

"They left you here alone?" It was beyond him that they would leave a pregnant woman alone, much less a recently widowed one.

"I just wanted a few of days by myself before I went to stay with my friend to go into confinement. I insisted. I didn't realise what the pain was. I left it too long. I couldn't get help."

"The unmarked grave? Oh Meg!"

"I blamed myself, but the Doc said he had so many problems that he would never have lived. His back was open… his face had a hare-lip, and Doc said he had heart problems as well. It was so pointless to carry a life that would never live. It was his one joy: that he had a baby that would carry his name after he left. Even at the end… that little baby I was carrying was the thing that made it okay for him. His name was to be Alistair David. Or Alison Daisy… that is a Scottish name too. Alistair never knew his son didn't make it. I let them both down."

"Meg… how can you know these things? Perhaps like you said, the comfort of that idea was a good thing… for Alistair. For you… too."

"But he was so damaged. I didn't keep him safe. I felt so alone…" She shivered from the horror of the memory.

"You're not alone. Not now. I'm here," he murmured over her trembling body and she buried herself in his arms, wracking with sobs that also had never been cried.

She eventually stood up and poured herself another

drink and washed her face. "I went to my friend's place for a while… to recover. No one expected me to come back here, but I had to. Everything we planned… it wasn't finished. I put the legal papers aside to look at later. I never did, that's all."

"Meg. It's kind of important. You should have attended to this."

She hedged. "I couldn't decide how to. I don't have any family. It was meant for our son!"

"Did you consider that if Grossman found out Petrea Downs is unsecured, you could have had a very serious accident? Nothing like the frustrations he's thrown at you up to now."

"Accident? Frustrations? What do you mean?"

"He's tried wooing you with flattery. When that didn't work, he went to wearing you down. When you didn't fold, he turned up the heat. To prove you can't do it alone… that you needed him."

"That's preposterous. He was always here to help me. He offered support. He was the only friend I had."

"Yeah. Wasn't that convenient? The fences are down… and he comes over. Your cartwheel breaks… he's here to help fix it. The dingos get into your chook pen, and the new calves are taken…"

"How do you know this stuff? How could any of this be true?"

"You've mentioned them. The common factor is

always the ever-present Everett Grossman."

She gasped. "The boundary fire! He was here so quickly."

"At the risk of sounding bitter and jealous, I'm pretty sure his overtures are more about your property boundaries than your unparalleled beauty."

"You seem confident of that. He might admire my beauty."

"Oh, I know you are beautiful... and I'm also sure he admires it. Like he admires his kept woman in town."

"Huh." She stood up as the kettle whistled and took it from the fire. "Once I would have defended his honour, but now I find that kind of sordid accusation not at all surprising."

"Yet he didn't count on you being independent, resourceful, stubborn, smart, capable, as well as beautiful."

She stared at him. "Go on..."

"To start with, having a felon was another problem you had to deal with. Me not getting a court hearing – that had nothing to do with keeping me out of prison. No one knows me. But me... me becoming an ally? That was unexpected, and when Grossman realised he had left it too long, the backlog cleared and I'm potentially facing court."

"That's ridiculous. Of all the intrigue and schemes of treachery I've ever heard..."

"Think about it..."

"The cattle? He was behind that?"

"I don't know for sure. I wasn't told where the money was coming from. But we were to be paid, and not just by the sale of the cattle... there was also a purse. An attractive one at that. I'm not sorry it brought me here though. I'd thank him for that."

"You? Is this another ploy for Petrea Downs?"

"Me? I don't want your land!"

"How do I know that?" She shook her head staring at him. "You've said yourself Petrea Downs has some of the best prime pasture around."

"And some of the poorest tracts of rocky ridges as well. But that doesn't matter. If you are here, I stay... so I don't need my name on any deed. If you are not here, I have no reason to stay. I'd go."

"You'd just leave?"

"Without you, Petrea Downs will lose its soul. What you did... staying here... that is so gutsy. I don't have that in me. Every sod, every blade of grass, every post... would remind me of you. I couldn't do that. I wouldn't do that."

"I might want you to remember me... to have this."

"Might? Yeah. See, that tells me there is still a niggling doubt that suggests I'm after your money, or your property. One sure fire way to know I'm not, is to eliminate it as an option."

"But what if we had a son... or a daughter?"

"I'd probably get someone to lease it until they are of age. Huh. That wouldn't work, because I'd never trust them not to let it run down. I don't know what I'd do. It's a tough call." He closed his eyes.

"Ben, I want to get rid of the doubt. I really do…"

He looked up at her. "Then we sort it so that you do."

"But how?"

"We'll go into town tomorrow. You are doing this."

"But you miss the point. I have no family. No one."

"Surely you have a niece or a great-uncle or second-cousin-twice-removed you can leave it to." She shook her head. "McGregor? Does he have family?"

"Alistair's older brother died. There is a nephew."

"McGregor's are not known for their longevity then."

"The child's mother has remarried. Quite well. He would be well catered for."

"A spoilt brat is all this place needs."

9.

Ben finished the evening chores and headed up to the house. Meg had already cooked their meal and they sat together afterwards without saying much. She smoothed out a letter that had been delivered and pushed it over towards Ben. It contained a list of every service Grossman had ever offered with a monetary value attached to it. The mending of the cartwheel; wages for the men who fixed the boundary fence; stockmen who rounded up strays; the services of the maid who came to tend Ben while she drove the cattle into the saleyards. The list went on. Meg shook her head bewildered. "I thought he was offering neighbourly support for a friend who needed help!"

"That ain't a friend," Ben said frowning into his coffee mug.

"I never agreed to terms for any of this! I understood it was a favour. It will take a long time to be free of this, but I can't have my place hanging in the balance over the services of a housemaid. I'll just have to factor it in. I have to get rid of this." She put down her cup and swallowed awkwardly. She paused, not sure how to proceed. "When we went into town, I didn't think you would do that. But you did. I've thought about it over and over. I still don't understand why. It seems just as perplexing as this. Grossman is demanding payment not just for the official loan, but for all sorts of services rendered. He sold them to me as good-will. Yet for you… it seems like the exact opposite. Can you really want nothing at all?"

"Oh Meg, I want something. You know it. But I told you: without you, this land means nothing."

"But how can you say that? This place has been my link to Alistair. It has kept him alive for me."

"Meg? He ain't alive," he said. He closed his eyes and regulated his breathing. "Perhaps that's it. Perhaps I want to be connected… now… without the past between us."

She slapped the table and got up and paced. Everything felt so tangled. When she was staring down Grossman, even through the fog of her recovery, her plan had been so clear. But now it was confused and uncertain again. "Oh, I don't know! I'm not sure I know what I mean."

"Meg? I love you. Not your land: you. That's why I had that document drawn up like that. So that you would know it. I can't change the law that says a husband gets his wife's property, but I can determine who gets mine. My will defers back to you and your wishes. If I outlive you, there is one very spoilt little nephew who will be just bursting at the seams at his good fortune." He got up and stood in front of her. He reached out and steadied her restlessness. "This is the same as what Alistair did. If we have children, Petrea Downs will be held in trust for them and they get to choose what they do with it when they come of age. Meg, please… I am asking you to marry me. Will you? Marry Me? Not because of what you have lost, or could lose, but because of what we gain by being together. You signed the declaration of intent, but I'm not going to try and hold something over you, Meg, no matter how respectable it sounds on paper. You can always pull out." He wished he had left that last bit unsaid. Why would he present that as a legitimate option?

"I… I… I feel disloyal. Perhaps that is what I mean. I'm scared I will lose him. He was a good man. There is no one else to remember him like that. It is so unfair that he would disappear without a trace!"

"Oh." He looked down at his work-callused hands and realised he had no answer for that. No signed piece of paper would fix that. He went to the door and picked his hat off the peg. "What you had with him was good. I admit I'm jealous of that because it is something I'll never be part of. No one can ever take that away from you, Meg. Hell, I wouldn't want to." He closed his eyes and took a breath. "I guess you will know if… when… you are prepared to try this… try me. But you have to do that, Meg. I can't sign that away. You know I would if I could. So, when you are ready… let me know. I will be waiting." And he walked out into the dark. The cool night air stung his eyes, dry and gritty from the disappointment.

He lay on his bunk; the little lamp on the table flickered dimly. He couldn't be bothered to get up and trim it. It would soon burn out anyway. He looked at the photograph in his hand, and imagined it was Meg standing beside the groom. What would it be like to have her by his side like that? What if he would never be an option because he was not Alistair McGregor? Would he always be caretaking another man's dream, and another man's wife? He said he would wait, but now he was not sure. Perhaps that was something he could not, would not, do forever. If she could not let McGregor go, he would make himself get on his horse and ride and never turn back.

He dozed fitfully. He despised everything about Grossman: his presumptuous accounting, his manipulative agendas, and his self-absorbed prescription of a set time for the mourning of widowhood. He was trying to work out how long. How long does it take to grieve? What if this was something she would always carry? What if she wasn't willing to bring her grief with her into their marriage? Did it have to be finished before she could move on? Couldn't this also be a road to healing? Would they stay separated on two different sides of a very deep ravine forever?

The questions were smothering him. How could he ever breathe again if that was what she chose? He stirred to the horses restlessly neighing and stamping. His eyes still smarted in his sleep. Then he realised the smell of smoke. He startled awake to find smoke filtering an orange glow of flames filling the front of the stables. He ran towards the door but flames quickly blocked the passage. He grabbed the axe from the workbench where he had been grinding it on a stone, and coughing he smashed a hole in the wall of the back stall. He released his horse. He went to Meg's saddle mare, and the other stock horse and led them out. He went back for the cart pony, skittish and shying in the stall. He quietly spoke her down and led her limping to the opening in the stall and let her go.

The fire was advancing fast. He looked at it, despairing, but already the rafters were running alight with flames. All he could manage was to grab some tack, bridles and their saddles and a box of tools.

He ran to wake Meg. The house was flickering in the light of the stable fire as he stormed inside. Meg was lying on the floor, tied and gagged. Her eyes wild, her cheeks wet, and her hair dishevelled.

"Did they touch you? Did they hurt you?" He shouted, the fire still roaring in his ears, and he fumbled as he untied her arms and legs and pulled off the gag.

She fell into his arms sobbing. "You're okay! You're okay."

"I'm okay. We're okay," he said as he searched her face. "Did they touch you?" he asked again.

She shrugged. "They broke in. Tied me up." She shuddered involuntarily as she rubbed her head where she had hit the floor as they dragged her out of bed.

"Who were they?" he asked.

"I don't know. It was dark."

He looked across at the letter on the table. "This is no random attack. This has Grossman all over it! A fire after a debt collection notice is a strong message."

She shuddered again, and he held her as they walked out onto the verandah. The stable was a fierce inferno. She saw the horses' skittish silhouettes at the water trough. The voices of those men filtered through her thumping headache; promising in an ominous growl that she would be an inconsolable widow once more. They could not know that only three hours earlier she had settled in her heart that remarriage was not for her. She couldn't do it. But as she lay there, facing that horrifying possibility, only one way seemed reasonable, or necessary, or urgent. If she were to be a widow again, she would first take the privilege of being married. Then they kicked her, and she had passed out.

Meg stared at the stable roaring violently in gold flames and a cascade of sparks gushed into the night sky as the roof collapsed. She realised that so much of Alistair was in that shed. He had built it. He worked there. And now it was turning to ash. Ashes to ashes. Dust to dust. Perhaps it was a sign.

She pulled back from Ben's arms as he held her and looked into his eyes. His face was smeared with dirt and char and he smelt of smoke and singed hair. "Yes," she said firmly.

His eyes went murderous, and for a moment she was scared by the fury she saw there. "By every fibre in my body they will pay for this! Grossman is not as untouchable as he thinks!"

"No. No. Ben! Not me. I'm not hurt. Bruises and a headache where they hit me, that's all. They tied me up so I could not warn you. You asked a question last night. To that question my answer is "Yes"."

"What question? What do you mean?" Did he dare hope?

"Yes. That question. My answer is yes."

"Meg? You will marry me?"

"Yes."

He steadied himself as he enveloped her in an embrace. "Oh! Are you sure now? No doubts?"

"Plenty. But the idea of losing you, that is horrifying. If we have to leave... that's what we do."

"Leave? And let Grossman strong-arm his way in here? I'm not inclined to hoist a white flag just yet!"

"You want to stay? They tried to burn you alive!"

"Yeah. And here I am still." And they kissed against the backdrop of fire, and pain, and relief, and of the gift that it all was.

They walked towards the stables and watched it burn. The south wall collapsed. The fire was contained, and all that was needed was the vigilance to whack out the occasional spot-fire from flying embers with a saddlebag Ben dunked in the water trough. It was furious.

It wasn't long before the fury abated. Ben gathered

the horses and put them in the holding yards. The cart pony was badly limping. He would look at his leg in daylight. He leant against the railing fence.

"Meg, how did Alistair handle Grossman? This can't be new."

She shrugged before she answered. "I don't really know. He thought of Everett as his neighbour. He didn't think badly of him. But then, Alistair never thought badly of anyone. Yet he never took any help either. No loans. No favours. Just stayed polite, and dug a lot of post-holes for this holding yard when he was feeling the pressure."

"You don't think that they... well you know... murdered him, do you?"

She shook her head. "No. I don't think even I can blame Everett Grossman for my husband developing tumours. Or that Dr Mansfield's treatment could do no more. We did everything he told us."

"So that was the fight of his life... not Grossman. That's how you knew what to do? You had a compulsory traineeship in nursing."

She nodded. As the last of the shed collapsed in on itself, they walked back to the house. It was over so quickly.

Ben took the notice on the table and smoothed it out in the lamplight. He inhaled deeply, the smell of smoke in his lungs. "This lists the debts that Grossman thinks he is due. He is using his tough voice because he wants you to think you're unprotected. Tomorrow we go back to town.

We get married. We go to the bank for a loan and pay out these debts. That will be quicker and cleaner than fighting the falsehood of all this."

Meg stared at him. "Except for one thing. A bank is not going to lend us any sort of money. I've tried. It's why I ended up going to Grossman when things got behind."

"We try again. Things look better on paper now. And if not… there might be another way. Right now, I'm taking a blanket. This is the last night I'm sleeping on the floor." And in the remaining hours just before dawn, he slept like a baby.

10.

Meg signed the paper and sighed. It was done. With all her willpower she tried not to remember her wedding with Alistair. Her beautiful gown; the ceremony in the church; the congratulations from family and friends; the lavish gifts; the celebrations that continued into the night; the honeymoon, and the innocence of believing it would last forever. She looked across at Ben as he leant over the register. She wondered if she would even feel married, because it just seemed like they were signing documents to open a bank account.

That was before they actually went to the bank across from the courthouse to address the loan issue. They produced the certificate and their ledgers. They spoke with the manager. He shook his head. Ben reassured and argued and reasoned. Eventually, Ben stood up and gathered their papers into a leather pouch, resigned to this rejection. He opened the door for Meg and walked outside. He paused under the shop-front awning, leaned against the post, and looked down the dust blown street, reflecting on their next move.

Meg also tried to gather her thoughts. Of course, the bank would not be moved. It was no surprise. But where to now? She walked back and forth in front of the bank trying to drive that smothering feeling of inertia away. As she turned, she bumped into a pedestrian and the pouch she was holding knocked out of her hand. He apologised hastily and helped her pick up a couple of scattered papers, and then hurried on his way. As she stood up, Grossman was standing there in his grey town suit. "Miss Meg! What a pleasure!" he said tipping his hat.

Meg jolted and stared. Ben didn't move except for adjusting the brim of his hat just a little lower over his eyes.

"Is everything okay? You seem a little distracted."

"No, no. Everything is not alright!"

"Oh? Is there any way I can be of assistance?"

"Sure. You can withdraw your ridiculous claims that I owe you money for the services of a housemaid."

"Oh Meg. You cannot seriously think that I would neglect to pay my workers correct wages. I could never expect that they would offer these assistances without appropriate compensation. And it all adds up… as you well understand. But, should you change your mind on my offer of marriage of course that would all change."

"Marry you? Under the threat of blackmail with bankruptcy? You might as well hold a gun to my head. You cannot be serious!"

"Oh, Meg I have tried to be reasonable. I've tried to tell you of my affection. I have to show you that if I am not your suitor, I am…"

"Hello neighbour," said Ben stirring from his possie by the awing post, tilting up the brim of his hat with his finger.

"Harker! What are you doing here?" He eyed a light bandage covering the burn on his forearm visible where he had rolled up his sleeves. "I heard there was a shed fire."

"You heard? Well news does travel fast. Damn business though. Unlucky accident."

"Unlucky?" He narrowed his lids.

"Yeah. Local rats must have knocked over my lamp. I left it burning when I fell asleep. It happens."

"Oh… suppose it does. So, you'll be leaving then?"

"No. I'm staying around. In case those rats cause more damage."

Grossman lowered his voice. "You won't ever work in this town. Even though you weren't charged, mud sticks. I'll see to it."

"Appreciate the concern, I really do, but don't trouble yourself on our account. We are just in town for the day… sorting out some family business. I see that you have met my wife."

Grossman physically jolted. He quickly looked at Meg's hand and stared at the simple wedding band on her finger. "You married this no-body low-life felon?"

She went a stood by his side. "I am done with my widow-weeds. It was something you recommended many times. I see now that it was good advice."

A bright red flush ran up his neck, and he stormed into the bank slamming the door. Ben lifted Meg's chin and smiled. "And that is why I love you."

She shook her head self-consciously. Ben straightened and wiped his hands on his moleskins. "Meg, I was hoping this wouldn't come up, but I'm thinking this is going to be the only immediate way to get Grossman off our back." He took a deep breath. "I'm going to introduce you to my father."

She spluttered and took a step back, staring at him in disbelief. "I'm sorry, did you say 'father'?"

He looked at her soberly without the slightest trace of amusement. "Yeah. I did."

"Why didn't you say you had family in town? Ben, we were married just two hours ago! How are you going to tell them I am now your wife?"

"I think… "*Meet my wife*" should cover it."

"You are perfectly serious! I cannot believe it. This is not right."

"We don't have a lot in common, that's all."

"Isn't being 'family' fairly substantial common-ground? What about your mother? Is she here too? I'm sorry Ben, I need some time to think about this."

"My mother is not around. And we don't have time to deliberate about whether I was right or wrong not to mention it. Right now,… we need his money. Loan only. And this is our best shot for immediate cash." She stared at him horrified. "Meg, are you with me on this?"

"Do I have a choice?"

"You always have a choice. But I think this is the best one given that stiff-necked accountant in there."

"Oh, my goodness. What have I done? Can you even tell me who your father is?"

"William Benjamin Madsen. Lives up on the hill."

The heat radiating off the street made her feel faint. "Madsen? Bill Madsen, the stock and station agent?"

"That's him."

"That man is your family? How is that possible?"

"Can't choose your blood-kin, that's all."

"You are not seriously going to ask Madsen for a loan?"

"Ain't my first preference. Thought that was obvious."

"He has never once given a decent price on my stock… and he charges like a wounded bull for everything else."

"That's his reputation: tight and mean."

"Well, he's not going to lend us anything, then is he?"

"I'm going to play the family card."

"What does that even mean? You've already said you aren't close. I thought his only son was Will."

"Well, now you know what we're dealing with."

"Huh. I bet I don't even know the half of it."

Ben opened the door for Meg and strolled into the store. He looked around the shelves listlessly, choosing his words. A youth came over to them and stood there rather awkwardly, all limbs and acne, waiting until he was acknowledged. Ben looked him up and down and felt pity stir in his belly. "Will Madsen, isn't it?"

The boy grinned as if he liked the notion of being famous. He stood up a little taller. "How can I help you, Sir?"

"I was wondering if I could have a word with your father?"

"Oh. Well, I think so. Who will I say?"

"Someone who knew an old friend... Elizabeth Perkins."

He nodded and retreated out the back. In a few moments, Bill Madsen appeared at the door. He was one of those enviable middle-aged men whose good looks matured: the tinges of grey around his temples looked sophisticated, but there was the coldness of steel in the blue of his eyes that made Meg cringe.

Madsen stood there, looking straight at Ben. He said nothing for a while, and then he pasted on a smile and came forward. "So, you're the young man who says you know Betty Perkins?"

He nodded. "I do. Quite well."

His eyes narrowed momentarily. "Oh. Well, that has been a while. Why don't you come out the back where we can talk without being disturbed? Will! Keep an eye on the shop and don't interrupt me now Boy. And restack those boxes out the front. They look like a dog's breakfast."

Ben followed him to the door of his adjoining office space. "Thank you, Mr Madsen. This is my wife, Meg Harker."

Meg flinched. She had not heard her married name spoken out loud. She gathered herself and curtsied.

Madsen looked her up and down. "Well, Well. Mrs McGregor. So, you've finally taken off the black. I've always thought your good looks were wasted on lonely cows and cantankerous horses."

"Perhaps I attract lonely and cantankerous," she said in measured tones, and Ben chuckled drily as Madsen stepped aside and ushered them into his office, offering them a seat on the lounge.

Bill closed the door firmly and then poured some drinks. "So, to what do I owe the pleasure of your visit? Mrs Madsen is visiting at the Women's League, so we can talk frankly," he said pointedly. Madsen swirled his drink and paused. "How did you say that you know Betty Perkins?"

"I didn't say. She is my mother." Ben said nothing further for a long while.

Madsen looked up quickly and stared at him like an evil apparition. Meg glanced from one to the other, and awkwardly gazed at the carpet mat on the floor in between times. Eventually he cleared his throat and said, "I am a busy man. There must be some purpose to your visit."

"No doubt." Ben sipped his drink slowly. "You know… I've wondered almost all my life what it would be like to sit in your lounge, and sip your drinks, and eat your food. And now that I am here, I have got to say, it is monumentally disappointing."

Meg gagged on her drink and swallowed.

Bill gulped and emptied his glass. "What is it you want?"

"I'd love for my mother not to have gone through what she did. But all the wanting in the world is not going to change what happened. So instead, what I need is a loan. The terms will be mainly based on my ongoing lack of interference in your neat little life. Young Will need never know he just met his brother. Your wife need never know that her beloved son is neither your first-born nor the uncontested heir to your empire. Yes… I have the letter you wrote to her. I've shown it to solicitors… and they believe that the paper has grounds."

"Don't you threaten me boy. I have watertight legals at my disposal. You will never win a fight with me."

"I have no intention of fighting you. The thing is… people can lose quite significantly, without any sort of fight at all. Elizabeth Perkins can testify to that. She lost just about everything… except her dignity. Even you couldn't flog that, although you gave it a good solid shot."

"Little Betty. I told her. I told her we could sort it. Stubborn thing. Refused! Couldn't move her on it. That isn't my fault. I tried to fix it."

"Telling me you wanted it 'fixed'... is somewhat akin to finding a contract was put on my head. Not feeling the family affection."

"There is no affection you filth! You come in here looking like a vagabond. You have people trying to keep your rotting carcass out of prison, your head out of a noose. Yes. I know about that. Who's going to believe the likes of you?"

"Oh, I am well aware. I have no illusions of grandeur. See, that paper may not prove anything at all, except one very tiny detail. Miniscule almost. Paternalism. It is dated and addressed to my mother. It has your signature... very bold hand you write with, even at eighteen. And that... as insignificant as that detail seems, *that* could create a whole lot of havoc in your tightly sealed up world. What a mess! To have those sorts of disreputable ties connected to your family... to your business. I even have the dropped charges of cattle-duffing to add colour to the indignity of it all. Does Mrs Madsen know about your indiscretions?"

"Damn it boy. How much do you want?"

Ben named the amount, and the terms he wanted. And then added. "I thought a wedding gift might also be a nice gesture. Being recently married and all. For your son and his bride."

"Keep your voice down. Is this what you need for your silence?"

"Silence? I'm not making demands. This is a business transaction... fair and square. And a gift, based on the regard you have for kinfolk. That is all."

Madsen went to his desk and unlocked the bottom drawer. He pulled out a wad and counted off the loan amount. He added some extra notes. He wrote it down as Ben instructed: the amount and the terms, including what was 'the gift'. They all signed and dated it at the bottom.

"Anything else?"

"Well, no I don't think so. I'm just excited that we will be doing business as family now. Cattle sales: with you overseeing the lots. It is good knowing that we will get a fair price and honest dealings, as kin from now on. And a family discount at the store, should just about put things in the price-range of reasonable, so we do appreciate you applying that."

"Blackmail and extortion."

"I prefer to call it fair and sensible. Long overdue."

Meg curtsied and Ben put his hat back on his head, and they left very sedately. They spoke to the solicitor to act on their behalf and then got on their saddle horses and rode home.

Meg sat on the settee on the verandah. Her mind was breathless with what she had witnessed. She watched him walk across from the holding yards. She had married a stranger. As Ben stepped up, he paused and looked at Meg sitting there, deep in thought.

"You look lovely this evening Mrs Harker. That was quite a day we had."

"Nothing like I imaged. I hardly know who you are."

"Here's the thing: we have a lifetime of discovery ahead of us."

"Why didn't you tell me Madsen was your father?"

"Ain't my father. Just because he did the deed, doesn't make him my Pa. My father's name was Jensen Harker. He's the one who raised me and my brother. He's the one who put my mother's life back together. I had a father Meg, and Madsen ain't it. I know that now."

"Then what was that about?"

"Getting the loan."

"None of it was true?"

"The guts of it is. Mum was working for Madsen's father at the shop when she left school. She was just past sixteen when she got pregnant to the boss's son. Bill was eighteen. The family left town when he refused to marry her. Jensen Harker gave my mother an offer of marriage before we were born. He was a fair bit older, recently widowed with a couple of teenage kids of his own who were not much younger than her. So, she married him. And yet Mum always told me she was blessed; always insisted she had a good life. Dad had a heart attack when I was nineteen and Ma was already sick. But before the end she told me everything and gave me the letter that Madsen had written. She never responded to it, but she kept it. I wanted to see who he was; what he was like. That's why I came here to Farthing to find work."

"So that thing about wondering your whole life who he was?"

"I'd call it poetic license... for effect. Knew nothing about Madsen until Ma told me. Didn't even have a hint. But these past three years have *seemed* like a lifetime in some respects."

Meg breathed deeply. "So, where's your brother living then?"

Ben grinned. "I'm not thinking about my brother just now, Mrs Harker," he said softly.

Meg blushed. He took her hand and stood her to her feet. "I believe there is a tradition about carrying one's bride across the threshold. Is that something you would be open to...?"

"I guess so," she said, nodding faintly.

And he swept her up into his arms and he kicked the door closed behind him as they stepped across the threshold into their new life.

11.

Meg opened her eyes. She looked across at Ben, lying beside her, breathing regularly in sleep. She went over yesterday in her mind, reliving every moment. She was stunned by Ben's audacity. There was a boldness she had not noticed before and she felt a shiver of fear. What if this was all a huge mistake? Then she recognised, there had been moments where there was evidence of that unmasked brashness… like the execution of the duffing incident.

And his insistent self-hiring.

His decisive action to write up their wills.

And his confident dealing with the fire, and the debt notice.

And his unwavering patience with her hesitation.

Had she married him because she thought he would be pliable and easy and convenient? A cheap farm-hand? She was pretty sure that if she had made those assumptions, they were now rendered void.

She traced the scars on his shoulder with her finger. She was familiar with every raised line. She felt a stab of shame at how much she had wanted him to suffer, made him suffer. Yet he never mentioned it.

He opened his eyes as he felt her touch on his skin. She kissed his scars. "Sorry…"

"You're sorry you married me, or saved my life? I'm

not, on either account."

"No... I..."

He rolled over and looked into her eyes, the flecks of blue washing in a sea of green. "Shh. It was a terrible way to burst in on your life, Missus Magdalena Evelyn Harker. Can we agree that was a rather unconventional start to married life? Can we go on from here?"

"I feel like..." She shrugged and didn't even know how to articulate what she wanted to say.

"Mrs Harker..." he said with a smile as he kissed her neck. He just liked saying it. "Mrs Harker, I moved here to chase some demons, and in the process met a beautiful angel. I had no concept my life could be so purposeful until I came here."

"When did you know that you loved me?"

"Hmm. It's sort of not a glamorous moment."

"I'm up for it."

"I was feeding the dogs the carcass of a wallaby you shot. That wallaby just fell on the spot. Never moved an inch. It's the same every time you shoot a snake, or a dingo or get a rabbit for dinner. Doesn't matter what it is; never seen you miss. I remember thinking you were damn scary with that gun of yours. I have no doubt that if you wanted me dead, I would be. That kind of rang a bell for me. I was trying to remember when I had heard someone talking about a girl who could shoot like that. It was then I remembered that conversation with Alistair at the pub. I went looking and found a photograph of you both. It was him. You were that Meg. I felt sick that I ended up hurting the person who inspired him to fight; you were the person that he wanted safe. I had a long look at myself. It was then I wanted to make amends."

"Huh. All I wanted was for you to leave."

"To start with, I spent a lot of time thinking about how to get away. Doc Mansfield told me straight why I needed to stay put. By the time I realised I had a complete change of heart I didn't think it would ever come to anything, because you loathed me so intensely."

"That's a little harsh."

"Am I wrong? I thought that if you had any idea what I was hoping for, you probably would have shot me again... only more permanent like."

She grinned. She couldn't actually deny the possibility of that.

He continued, "You know those spectacles of coloured glass that you can get at country shows? Alistair's words became like that... they tinted everything I looked at. I wanted to be that guy he talked about. I realised that was how I was raised. That was the way my Dad fought for my Mum. He used what he had to fight for her; to keep her safe."

"The first time I noticed you... like, really noticed you... was when I heard you and Grossman talking. The way you stood up to him... there was no fear. There was something in your tone that shocked me. Not arrogance or malice, but I knew he didn't intimidate you. I couldn't hear a word, but you spoke as his equal. You never told me what you were talking about."

Ben leant up on his elbow. "Hmm. They say curiosity killed the cat. I'm not inclined to jeopardise my newfound..."

"A cat gets nine lives. I'll be okay."

"Alright then. I saw how flustered you were when you left. So, I took some wood inside to check it out. Grossman was preening himself in the mirror above the sideboard like some dressed-up cockatoo. He pulled out this ring, and he flashed it around, showing it off like it was the crown jewels. I wanted to deck him so hard and vomit all at once. You're too good for him. So, I asked how Josephine Barns was, just to rile him up some. He thought that little secret was safely out of your reach. He got nervous and tried to pay me off. I told him that if he had money to throw away, it would be put to better use to buy you a decent ring. He offered to get my charges dropped. I said the only thing he should be dropping was the line-up of women who thought they were going to be his missus. He should have the decency to pick one and leave you alone. He threatened me with the usual stuff: a hanging, life in prison, work-gangs, and such. But then he got all lofty and superior and said none of that mattered because he had been courting you for nigh on two years. He said he'd set you up to trust him and it was all but done. Smug scum. That's when I decided I wouldn't stand by and do nothing. I'm not much, but hell, I'm better than that."

"But that is when you banished yourself to the shed. You never stayed in the house after that... except when I was sick. You went further away... not closer."

"To be in the running I had to get the idea out of your head that I was your house-boy."

"That's absurd. I never thought of you as my house-boy!"

"I was an anonymous felon who was invisible and only became useful because I'm good at stock work. I didn't want to be convenient Meg. For you I need to be indispensable."

"I still don't get the urgency to live in the stables with the mice and the farm-cat."

"And a fairly large carpet snake. But it worked. You started to see me differently. You started to ask what I thought. When you kissed me though; that was the clincher. I was done for."

"I think for me... it was the photograph. That and the fire. I didn't realise what I was feeling until I thought you were married to someone else: it just bowled me over. I was shocked by what came out of my mouth. But the fire... when I thought you were..." she gasped and shuddered, reliving a horror that was still too close and too real.

"Shh…" He kissed her and held her and then lightened his tone. "You know, I had this thing with the photo that I'd use when girls were getting too close. I'd work it so that they'd accidently find the photograph. The decent ones would freak out. The others would shrug like it didn't matter… and then I would freak out. It was a great filter for me. I never actually expected you to go down there and find it. I panicked a bit, cause, I thought you might shut me out without hearing what it was. I never told anyone it was Liam's photograph before. That was a first."

"So, Liam is your brother?" He had a name.

"Yeah. He's not going to be happy he wasn't best man. We had this deal – to be there for the big moments. He'll get over it."

"We could've waited…"

"You said yes. What makes you think I would wait?"

Her smile clouded over. "Ben, I still miss Alistair. You do know that?"

"And I miss my parents. They are people who were important to us. Surely that's okay."

"But how can I just pretend I wasn't married to him?"

"Never said we had to pretend. You were married to him. Then you weren't. You didn't want it or choose it… but it happened. And now you are married to me. Life can throw us some pretty rough riders, and we get dumped on our ass. Our job is to get back in the saddle. You've done that every morning, you got up and didn't give up.

Hopefully now we get some smooth riding for a while."

"I want to believe that. But I feel split in half – like I'm being unfaithful to Alistair... and then being unfaithful to you for thinking that. Will I always live in this triangle?"

He saw the earnestness in her eyes, and he bit the silly quip on his tongue. "You know, I was so afraid you would never be able to be in this dual place as you adjust to not being his wife... and learn to be mine. I thought you would never do it. I'm grateful you chose to."

"Just before the fire... I had made up my mind that I couldn't do it. I decided never to remarry. Not just you. Anyone."

"Another unexpected turn on your resolve. Again, in my favour, so I cannot complain."

"Do you know what I don't get? How someone like you could ever stoop to duffing? You're... completely unexpected."

"Not my proudest moment. I was given an ultimatum, and I took it. I thought I had no choice. I thought a dodgy job was better than no job."

"Did you ever want to work for Madsen?"

He grinned. "We are playing twenty questions. This is a fun game."

"Then answer my question..."

"Madsen... yeah. I did a couple of jobs... never worked directly with him though, but I figured if his overseers are anything to go on... it's not a good match.

And the pay was pathetic. If he ever goes broke it will not be from paying decent wages that's for sure. He's the original cheapskate."

"When are you going to let Liam know he's been passed over while you were having a major life event?"

"I'll write to him. There are some things of Mum's that I'm hoping he'll bring up. Maybe like a wedding present for you. I was just planning on cashing them out. I left kind of quickly and Liam just packed it all up and put it in storage. They might come for a holiday... so you can meet the family. Would that be okay?"

"Perfectly! I want to meet this photogenic brother of yours."

"I told you... I'm much better looking. He has big ears. Oh. And by the way Mrs Harker, we are not working today... or tomorrow. This is our honeymoon weekend," and he kissed her neck again. "Mrs Harker..."

12.

The wagon pulled up and the driver stepped down. He lifted down his lady passenger and two kids followed, dusty and grumpy from road travel and they started squabbling over a toy that the young boy was trying to extract from his sister's hand.

A man passed and tipped his hat. "Looking sharp there, Ben…"

As the mother tried to placate the children, another passer-by spat on the ground near his polished boots. "Getting mighty big for your britches there Harker. Dressin' like a dandy."

A lady in a large hat stopped and smiled. Liam returned a smile, rather tentatively. "Who is your lady friend Benjamin? Someone we know?"

"I'm not sure you would know her. Have you met before?"

She glanced at her and then looked back at him and frowned. "I don't think so. Never seen her in these parts."

"Hmm…" He pursed his lips thoughtfully. "Then you probably don't know her." He tipped his hat and moved on, leaving the woman staring after him stammering.

He raised his brow as another gave a country salute. Liam was amused by the reactions his brother generated. He missed this. He made his way across the street to the postmaster general. There was a note pinned to the door informing customers they were closed for an hour or so to visit the nurse. There was no time to indicate whether he was at the beginning, or end of that break. He looked around and headed across to the Stock and Station agent. The bell tinkled as he opened the door. Will nodded and stood up taller. Whenever Ben Harker came in, he felt like a celebrity. The man had a way of making him feel important, like he knew significant stuff that was really helpful. Will looked at the felt hat the man held comfortably in his hand and suspected that his influence contributed to this marked improvement in Mr Harker's style. "Nice hat Sir. How can I help you today Mr Harker?"

"I was actually wondering if you could tell me the directions out to Petrea Downs."

The youth grinned knowingly. "This is a test isn't it, Mr Harker?"

"Well, it seems that you are the go-to-man around here. If people come in for directions I want to know they are accurate."

"Of course, sir. Take the Farthing-Kyramoor Road out of town. The second road on your right is East Road... down that for five mile; turn left onto Rocky Gully Road and the Petrea Downs' gate is three miles down on your left."

"That is impressive. As I knew it would be. Well done." He turned to leave when a sharp voice stopped him in his tracks.

"Harker!"

Liam turned on his heel to face the voice. A middle-aged man stood bulking out the doorway. He grunted and said, "You've got gall always poking your head in here. You know our terms."

"If I said it, I meant it."

"That's what you say. I've had enough of your honourable airs, making out you are so down-to-earth. Only thing more down to earth than you is a yellow-bellied snake. Look at you, coming in here all dressed up just to be ask'n stupid questions. I'm watching you Harker. I told you before, you won't win a fight with me."

Liam looked at his challenger with a raised brow. "Is a fight something I'd be looking for... in these clothes?" he said benignly as he brushed the cuff of his sleeve.

"As they say: the cut of his suit is the measure of the man."

Liam nodded. "Noted." Silence. He knew his tailor. He was confident about that.

Madsen cleared his throat. "Well then. As long as we understand each other."

"I am now 'suit'-ably aware I would say."

"You've got a smart mouth on you Harker. It'll get you into trouble one day."

"Sounds like you are in danger of being concerned for me."

"No risk. Now get your ugly mug out of here."

Liam waited until he turned away and put his hat on as he stepped outside before he allowed his grin to show.

The woman in the hat had returned with reinforcements and was talking with Ellen by the wagon. When he stepped up to her side, she continued without pause. "The Bible clearly talks about staying home for a honeymoon year. Whatever will Meg say about you bringing back another woman?"

"Well, probably less than you think. This is Ellen, Meg's sister-in-law."

"Oh? Of course. Well enjoy your visit Ma'am. Now don't be forgetting to remind Meg about that neighbourly get-together so that we can wish you newlyweds well. That girl has been through the mill. Sure, hope she knows what she's doing."

"Oh. Well, Ah... Excuse us ladies, we need to be getting home."

Ellen mustered the kids to climb up and shook her head as she settled in beside him. "Sounds like your little brother is still as charming, and as adept at getting into trouble, as ever."

Liam flicked the reigns; his amused grin was replaced by a frown. "Who would have thought that thirty-four minutes could make such a difference? His dress code has always been below par."

They sat around the table after dinner. The kids were tucked up in swags camping style. Meg looked at the brothers in the lamplight, and she could swear that if they had a similar haircut, she would struggle to tell them apart. Ellen leaned forward. "So, how did you two meet?" she asked sweetly.

Meg didn't pause. "I shot him." And then for a horrifying moment she regretted her country frankness. She feared she might have spoilt this family reunion. She glanced over at Ben and he was studying his drink, calmly munching on a biscuit.

Liam settled back in his chair. "See, now this is why women should not have access to firearms. I am lobbying for safer standards to be made obligatory in the crafting of arms."

Meg raised her eyebrows and Ben continued to drink unperturbed. "Oh no," he said without shifting his gaze from his biscuit, "you quite misunderstand. She did it on purpose." He was enjoying the shock that washed over their faces. He felt it was his job a shake some of that stuffiness out of Liam's well-cut clothes.

Ellen gasped. "On purpose? Whatever for? He could have been hurt!"

Meg wanted to leave this to Ben, but his smirk indicated that he resolutely was refusing to collaborate in cleaning up this mess. So, Meg smiled adoringly at her husband and said sweetly, "I didn't want him getting away."

A boyish grin lit up his eyes. "That is the actual truth. And here I am, captured forever!"

The visitors laughed and drank their tea. This was obviously a metaphor in their rather unconventional whirlwind romance. And so, Ellen reciprocated by sharing with Meg an account of their exciting romantic encounter on an exclusive social dance-floor.

Ben glanced at Liam and asked, "Did you bring it?" He nodded and patted his jacket inside pocket. Ben stood up. "Well I have a couple of apologies that are overdue. Liam. I'm sorry mate you were not here for my greatest moment, when Meg became my wife. And Meg I regret that I didn't have the opportunity to give you a ring worthy of our love before this. But I have waited so that I could rectify these lacks now. Meg would you wear my mother's ring with your wedding band? It would mean so much."

Meg tilted her head and nodded. Liam reached inside his jacket and pulled out a worn fabric box and handed it to Ben. He knelt down in front of Meg. He opened the case to reveal an exquisite gold filigree band with an enormous diamond, studded with a circle of emeralds and rubies. He looked up at her and said softly, "Meg, will you accept this ring? May it always represent my love encircling your life: precious and enduring and healing. As it represented those things for my mother... may it also be those things for us in our marriage. Thank you for being my bride."

He stood and held her hand to draw her to his side

and they kissed. Ellen sniffled misty eyed, and Liam cleared his throat. "Ben?"

"Don't interrupt me Bro... in the middle of something." When they finally released from their embrace, Ben looked over at his brother and grinned. "Guess you want to say a best-man speech or something?"

Liam shrugged. "Ben, you know I've always prayed for you, especially over these last couple of years. I want to pray a blessing on your marriage. Can I do that?"

"Damn, you are still hankering to do that preacher thing. Sure. Go your hardest. We need all the blessing we can muster."

"Gracious Heavenly Father. You have drawn Ben and Meg together... in unusual circumstances, and unlikely ways. I ask that You bless their union abundantly in every sphere of their lives. We ask this in the name of Jesus Christ our Lord, Amen."

Ellen brought out a box of fruit jellies that she wrapped as a hostess gift; she had anticipated them as a treat, rather than a wedding gift. For her it seemed embarrassingly inadequate and she apologised profusely. The sweets hadn't suffered too much in the trip and they had another round of drinks. Even though there was lots of catching up to do, they called it a night soon after, wearied from travel.

The next day the children rose early and bounced on Ben and Meg who occupied the swag in the corner of the room. As Meg rolled over to meet their boisterous greetings, she wondered how she would have felt if she had known that she would share the swag of the patient who laid wounded in this corner.

"Uncle Ben you have to teach me to crack a whip again. I've forgotten how to do it," sighed little Jensen distressed by the amnesia caused by a night-long sleep.

"You promised to show me how to throw knives," demanded Eliza.

Meg grinned. "You're quite the luminary." She lingered on the idea of Ben being around kids. No spinning tops or skipping ropes though; they went straight to whips and knives. She wasn't sure how comfortable Ellen would be with that.

Ben just laughed. "Okay. Okay. Jobs first. Then play." And he took them out to the wood heap, collected the eggs and milked the cow.

13.

Meg had done life alone for so long that she found having others around required a fair bit of effort. She couldn't believe how worn out she felt. That was confusing. She had been looking forward to her visitors so much, but now they were here, it was draining every ounce of her energy. When Ben had said there were some things of his mother's that he wanted Liam to bring, she was kind of expecting a vanity set of lace doilies for her dressing table, or a handmade quilt, or perhaps a china teapot. Instead they were presented with a wagonload of antique furniture; quality household furnishings including boxes of Manchester and chinaware. There were even a couple of trunks of clothes, a little dated, but tasteful in their style.

"This ain't all of it Meg. Ellen picked out some of the pieces that she thought might appeal."

"Ben, I thought you were destitute…"

"Well, I was living in a shed on a bushman's bunk with a cat, so I can understand why you thought that."

"Why didn't you tell me? You have obviously grown up with privilege. How can you be happy here with so little?"

"I needed to explore the idea of living independently… out of my own resources. That's not an unfamiliar idea for you. Heard you say the same thing to

Grossman many times."

"But I have never had the kinds of things you are used to."

"There is a reoccurring theme that suggests you cannot imagine how I would be interested in being your husband if I had the means to support myself."

"Why wouldn't you still want that kind of life?"

"Because I want the kind of life that captures my heart; stimulates my thinking. He grinned. "You know what you've done to my heart and you keep me thinking on my feet. Besides, when I found out about Madsen, I kind of figured that the Harker inheritance wasn't rightly mine anyway."

"You renounced your inheritance?"

"Well, no... I'm not an idiot. It will be useful. Nor am I the crown prince. It isn't an empire by any measure. But Dad was smart with money. He inherited a good amount, and he had a good job. He bought run down businesses and built them up. He worked as a town planner for a while, so he knew property and he invested well. He left us, and our sisters, a couple of places each."

"You have property?"

Ben shrugged and then nodded.

"Huh. That must have been amusing for you: that I accused you of coming after my land. Were you laughing at me the whole time?"

"No. Everything I said was true. It is still true. I ain't

in this because of what I can get out of you. Meg, you know that."

"It feels like nothing you said was real."

"I said I wasn't marrying you for your property. That is true."

"Why? Because it is not up to scratch? How is that different to the lies that Grossman told me?"

"You cannot be comparing me to that! The man is incapable of lying straight in bed. All he was ever doing was grooming you for a local takeover."

"It doesn't feel any different."

"I don't understand. When I was a disenfranchised criminal, you fell in love with me. But now that there is a possibility that I have a family that is as connected and as respectable as any McGregor, it feels wrong? I could steal your cattle again if that helps."

"Don't laugh about this. I'm serious. I have no idea who you are. I'm married to a stranger."

"No, you're not. I'm still that duffer you caught in the crossfire. Meg, it is still me. There are things about me you don't know. There are things that I don't know about you. It doesn't make our relationship invalid... just an adventure in discovering the unexpected."

"Well. Unexpected says it all! You're certainly that."

"That line you told Madsen about lonely and cantankerous: I thought that kind of hit the nail on the head. I might have undeclared income, but essentially I am still just a lonely cow-hand that is hard to get along with."

"I usually like to know what I am getting into."

"You knew the important stuff... and sometimes unexpected turns out to be better."

"How do you figure that?"

"Growing up I was kind of embarrassed that my dad was old, but now I know it meant he had time for us. He tutored us, read us books, taught us to ride, coached cricket, took us fishing and cheered us on. I think his parenting strategy was to keep us so busy we were too exhausted to get into trouble. Not that it always worked mind you."

Meg took a sip of water. This whole thing was upsetting. Her throat burned with reflux and she swallowed again. "Well he did well with you." And her eyes misted as she thought how proud she would be of her son if he had lived.

"Every time I meet Will, I think that could have been me: not ever feeling good enough; panting after anyone who has a good word to say; never able to do anything right. Rotten way to grow up."

"I imagine if you and Liam had grown up here in Farthing you would have been local celebrities terrorising the neighbourhood."

"Meg, Mum never got to tell Liam about Madsen. She wanted to, but in the end, she ran out of time. One of the last things she said to me was to go gently with my brother. She was worried he might not accept it the way I did."

"I thought you struggled with it."

"Yep. I did."

"But he doesn't know why you struggled?"

"Part of me doesn't want to tell him either. Him and Ellen... they work as they are. But I'm reckoning that sort of unsavoury background would unravel them. I haven't a clue how to tell him. They're not strong like you. The way you handled Grossman... such finesse. And at Madsen's you sat there so composed... took it all in. Didn't even blink."

"Ben, I think you still fail to appreciate that the Madsen thing was far less of a surprise than realising you grew up as a privileged, educated kid." She paused. How could she explain it? Perhaps she expected a criminal stooping to cattle duffing would have a marginalised, unfortunate childhood. Perhaps that seemed more reasonable than a well-to-do kid gone sour. It felt like every day she discovered that whoever she thought Ben was, it was not even close to the truth. "There's always more."

He looked at her and frowned. "Meg... are you upset about this or about our visitors staying on? Are you still okay with them being here? The kids are busy and noisy."

She sighed and sat back. "Guess I haven't properly got over that bout of fever. I feel exhausted. Ben, what are we going to do with all this furniture? We don't even have a shed to store it in."

"We'll go through it so you can put aside anything you

want. I'm thinking we will sell the rest. Probably send it back with Liam because he'll get a better price in town. I'm hoping we will be able to clear out most of Madsen's loan with this stuff."

"But don't you want to keep it? These are your mother's things."

"They are our things now. Some of it I would never sell... like the ring... and maybe the writing desk. She sat at it every night doing accounts. But we don't need most of it... so we can use it to get on top of things. I don't want to be obliged to Madsen any longer than we have to. Doing business with him is sleeping with a mulga snake. I was going to talk to you about building a shed. I thought about making it out of stone, that way we could do most of it for very little cost. That, and it won't burn down. I still think that area on the west boundary will make a good quarry. I'm taking Liam out there later to look at it." It was completely reasonable to him that all those ideas ran together so smoothly.

Meg shook her head. It seemed ludicrous how she was no longer the primary provider in this relationship. "You really don't care that you married a desolate, destitute widow?"

"Oh, you are wrong. I do care very much. And I am going to do everything in my power to see that she is neither of those things again."

"Excuse me... I'm going to be sick..." And she went

outside and reached the rail just in time.

"Ben?"

He looked up from the desk where he was writing. "Yep?"

She sat down and shivered. Fear gripped her heart. She shook her head as if untangling herself from a cobweb. "Ben what do you think about being a father?"

He finished blotting what he had written and put down the pen slowly. He turned to her with a question in his eyes. She nodded slowly. He sat back. "Really?"

Meg groaned inside. Of course, he would not be ready for this. Fear gripped her and she pushed back the tears that shimmered near the surface. Alistair had been so delighted... and heart-broken. She had hoped so much that this could be good news. She jumped up and went outside and was sick again.

Ben found her sitting on a stump in the wood heap. "Meg?" He stood there, uncertain. He suddenly felt an overwhelming sense of responsibility, and it frightened him to the core.

"Ellen twigged. It took so long to get pregnant before, I just wasn't thinking about this yet."

"Me neither."

"I wanted this to be happy news. We can't undo it. I

won't undo it." And even as she said it, she saw Madsen's arrogant eyes scorning Betty's decision. Would son, like father, also demand it be 'fixed'?

"What? No! Meg, I ain't disappointed. It's an idea that takes some getting used to; that's all. Never thought I was the husband type, much less father material. I'm not like Liam. A lot has changed in the last six months."

"For me too…"

"Oh Meg. Are you okay? I mean… you lost the other baby?"

"I'm okay… although I feel like the walking dead. I am kind of relieved it's just morning sickness."

"Oh."

"Ben. Are you going to stay? I need to know so I can make a plan."

"What? Meg, the baby is making you delirious!"

"I thought perhaps you'd want to go back to…"

"Cattle duffing? I don't think so. You have reformed my criminal ways. I am here to stay and don't be suggesting anything otherwise."

"Are you sure… because I…" She wavered and gagged and went as white as a sheet. Ben grabbed her and picked her up and carried her inside.

"Ellen!" Ben called as he laid her on the bed.

Dr Mansfield looked at her tongue and felt her glands. He noted that she needed to rest and take as much food as she could tolerate. It seemed that every time Meg tried to stand upright, she felt dizzy. If she did manage to sit up for any length of time, she would end up throwing up, and be compelled to lie down again. She could not remember her last pregnancy being so debilitating.

Ellen took Liam aside, and looked at him directly and said, "I would like to stay here while Meg is unwell." Liam frowned, and said nothing for a while. "Liam? I really want you to consider this."

"Well, given that she is pregnant, that will be months. There are lots of other things to consider. What about the firm, my work, the church, and our community obligations? We just can't stay indefinitely." He was annoyed she would ask this of him. "I thought you had a suitable sense of responsibility Ellen. You should realise these things cannot be put aside so easily."

Her eyes flashed and her lips went thinner. "Liam Harker, you have spent the last three years in a fever over your brother. You have always said that your father instilled in you both, to keep a watch on each other's back. You've blamed Ben for not adhering to that, but now it is your turn. Here you have a very practical way to put legs on that idea. You need to talk to Ben and see if he would like us to stay. They might not even want this. If they prefer us out of their hair, being newly married and all, that sort of answers the question."

"Ellen, I thought he wanted us to bring the ring and furniture because he was getting engaged. We get here and find he's already married and not even in a church. They were probably shacked up here together for goodness knows how long before that. It goes against everything we were brought up to believe. Do you think I want to throw my life away now just because he thinks he has found some sort of steadiness? Who knows how long it will last?"

"Liam! A few weeks does not constitute your life! Besides, he is your brother. You were always close. Why does that have to change?"

"I wasn't the one to change it. Ben did that when he left. I can't undo what's been done."

"But he's reached out again. You didn't even hesitate when you got his letter. Of course, they will get through: they have up to now. But I know I can help here. And so, can you."

"What about work?"

"What about it, Liam? You never take leave. This is the first time since our honeymoon and Eliza is five. What good is being a partner if you have no say? Just a few extra weeks. I expect it will settle down soon. That's all I'm suggesting. If you won't do it for your brother, I want to do it for my sister-in-law. I've never had a sister. I don't like it that we will be so far away. Meg is really suffering. This is a woman's time."

On her insistence, Liam wrote a letter to the firm and notified them of an extension on his leave. Ellen set to cooking meals and spent a lot of time hushing the children or sending them outside so not to disturb Meg who was feeling too sick to argue. They moved Meg back into the privacy of the bedroom, and then unloaded the four-poster bed from the cart and rearranged the living room so Liam and Ellen could sleep there.

Ben enlisted Liam to help with his plan for the work-shed, and he drew up a design to utilise Petrea Downs stone for the main structure. Then they marked out the site and started levelling.

Meg sat with Ellen on the verandah and watched them digging the foundation-trenches. "It doesn't seem that long ago that Alistair was doing the same thing for his shed. This has a very odd sense that I've been here before. It makes me feel that nothing is permanent; it just cycles around."

"But this building is made of stone. Surely that is different?"

"Perhaps it won't burn. But even stone is not indestructible."

"I wonder how you do this. It is extraordinary that you stayed here, after... well after... the funeral."

"I just never felt I had a choice."

"Liam has the same strong sense of duty. He is so entrenched where we are, but I wonder what it would be like to have our children grow up in a place like this. I envy your baby in a way."

"Yes, but you have family where you are."

"And now I have family here too."

That made Meg smile. She had never had someone say that before. Not really. Just Alistair.

Ellen started on a mission exploring job opportunities for a draftsman, town planners or architects, but a small town like Farthing had little need for these types of professional roles outside the occasional consultancy. Liam's choice to follow in his father's footsteps had never left them short of an opportunity up until now. On Sunday they went into town to attend church, and while they were gone, Ben sat with Meg on the verandah.

"How are you holding up?" said Ben staring out over the paddocks.

Everything at the moment seemed to be eroding on her strength. She steadied herself and tried to reassure Ben. "Yes, Ellen is such a blessing. I'm pleased she is here with me." She had few female friends in her life. The friend she had stayed with after the funeral moved away not long after she returned to Petrea Downs. Her world since had been dominantly isolated... or male. Still, she understood the role of the woman was to never whinge; never be dissatisfied; never hint that things were not blissfully smooth. But just now things were far from honeymoon perfect.

Their little hut was cramped with the extra family of

four. She felt sick from smells she had never even noticed existed before. Ellen insisted that she not do anything: no lifting, no stretching, no carrying, no pushing, no pulling. And each of these directives were accompanied with all sorts of maternal wisdom at what risk these behaviours would expose their baby too. She wondered if her need to work so hard had been the reason her son had been born the way he was. Not that she could do that again this time even if she wanted to. It seemed she was pinned to the bed with fatigue, and the times she was up, she was sent flying to the railing or grabbing a bucket.

So, while she sat and watched life on the farm go on around her, she had a lot of reflective time. And she found herself wondering, first and foremost, about her husband. How much was he like his brother really? Was there more history that he was closeting away? She looked at Ben leaning on the verandah rail gazing out over the holding yards. "Ben, did you ever try a profession like Liam?"

That avoided his question about how she was coping, but Ben went with it. "Liam was keen on the architectural internship ever since I can remember. He went to work at Dad's firm as soon as he could. I never wanted to. Dad organised for me to work with an accountant as a book-keeping clerk. It was like counting sheep. In fact, real sheep would have been a relief. I did what I had to do, but I was usually found asleep in the corner or under a desk somewhere by lunch. I think they didn't sack me straight away out of respect for Dad, and in the end, Dad arranged a job apprenticed to a master builder. That's what I was doing when Dad had his heart attack. Mum was already sick, and I stuck at it mainly to reassure her I was settled. But as she got worse, I was the one who stayed home with her on the bad days… and then pretty much all the time at the end. Liam couldn't get the time off."

"So, you also had an apprenticeship in caring for the incurable. That's why it didn't seem to faze you… looking after me when I was sick."

"Necessity is a great teacher. We had a nurse… mainly for night-shifts. Mum preferred me there."

"So, you became a master-builder then?"

"Never finished. Still it served a purpose. It was done when I was done."

"So, you don't regret not having a profession? Farming is hardly the same."

"Never did cattle work till I came out here. It was like coming home. It felt like it fitted."

"But Liam seems so certain about what he wants. You are the same age."

"Are we standing in the mirror comparing each other again? I gave that up when I was eight."

"Yes. But he seems so sure…"

"Liam is less sure than he looks."

"When are you going to tell him?"

He laughed. "You don't 'tell' Liam anything much.

He's... stubborn."

"Huh. You are the same after all. You do have to tell him about your Mum."

"I don't have to... and I probably won't unless my hand is forced. He doesn't need it."

"But doesn't he have a right to know?"

"I think he also has the right not to know. I'm trying to balance those two dimensions. I guess I'll know which one is the weightier when the time comes."

The brothers started the local stone-hewing crew working the Petrea Downs quarry. Liam's advice and his enthusiasm for its potential to contribute to a community development plan, gave Ben a marketing angle he was able to use. So rather than just quarrying enough stone for their own project, he also convincingly secured a couple of contracts with local builders. It was quickly becoming a steady income.

Meg was bemused that rock was potentially more profitable than the cattle she fought so hard to bring a return with. Her confinement was driving her to distraction, so Ellen took to showing her how to knit baby clothes, so she had some occupation to keep herself amused.

The idea of a community profile, even if it was a small community, was increasingly appealing to Liam over his invisible, back-room job at the firm. That the brothers functioned well together was indisputable. The project hardly seemed like work. They knew how the other operated and their skillset complemented each other hand-in-glove. It was evident that going into business together was a viable and desirable thing.

While the brothers were building the shed, they continued to beat out the particulars of the partnership. Ben hedged, and it was Liam who was increasingly the one presenting the case. Ellen was also keen. As Meg knitted and purled, she watched the progress of the building from the verandah and hoped that Ellen's eagerness for this current scheme was not misplaced.

Finally, Liam put down his tools and decided to have it out. "Okay. Let's do this right now. Why don't you want to work with me?"

"Why do you say that? I thought I was."

"Don't give me that. You've been running from this idea from the start."

"I was always faster."

"And I was always smarter, so tell me whether or not I uproot my family to do this. Ellen wants to. She thinks the country would be better for us as a family, but I'm not doing it unless you're in it one hundred percent."

"It really is your decision to make," he said evasively.

"I know all my arguments. I want to know yours. Why are you hedging?"

He paused and leaned on his shovel. "Well. I think you haven't forgiven me for leaving."

"I don't see how that has any relevance to this."

"You don't trust me to stick it out. Don't see that as a basis for a partnership."

"Well, consider this my grand gesture of putting it behind me!"

"If you think I'll pull the pin at any moment, the business will eventually fall on its face. Until that's different, it ain't going to work."

"I'm not marrying you Ben: its business. And I know you well enough to know you won't watch it fail. You can't. You were the youngest shift-boss that building crew ever had, and they had you managing the business side when you were staying home with Mum as well. Besides you're a Harker."

Yeah. About that. It was an opening he could drive a bullock dray through. He wondered why he wouldn't use it. "Always been your brother. That never changed. Even after mum died."

"I know you lost your bearings then Man... needed space. You were close to her." That was as generous as Liam had ever allowed, but he couldn't leave it at that. "Still... I was shocked that you pinged off like you did. It's supposed to be at times like that when family sticks together. It didn't seem to matter to you that it was hard for me too."

"You never asked why I needed to go. You just

assumed. You know squat."

"It's pretty obvious. What else could it be after losing Mum?"

"Well I was right to think you wouldn't listen. You weren't ready to hear it then. You're not now."

"You know what I think? I think you ran, just like you are now. That was damn inconsiderate given what we'd all gone through. In the space of six months we lost both our parents. Then I basically lost my brother too. That was hard. Harder than it needed to be. That's all I need to know!"

"You want hard? Okay then. I'll give it to you straight why it was hard." Ben stopped and looked at his brother. "But no… I ain't going to volunteer this. You have to want to hear it. So, if you ever change your mind on that, you let me know. Liam, I *will* tell you what it was about, but only when you ask for it."

That was said with enough soberness to give Liam pause. For the first time he considered the possibility that it wasn't just weak, unstable selfishness that caused Ben to abandon his family. He grunted as he picked up his shovel went back to work.

For days Liam worked mutely while Ben mortared and positioned stone as the walls started to take shape. They ate meals in silence, and all their usual banter dried up. Their extended holiday was fast coming to an end and Liam needed to make a decision one way or another. Ben was grateful for the space Liam's avoidance offered, but he knew that Liam had decided to hear him out. It would just be a matter of when.

14.

At smoko time Ben and Liam sat down amongst the piles of stone and sand and lime, with the wooden barrow, makeshift scaffolding and barrels of water that was their lunchroom. They boiled the billy, and tucked into their biscuits and damper that Ellen had sent the kids to deliver. They were not allowed to stay in amongst the construction and when they left Liam looked directly at Ben and he knew it was now. "Well?" Liam said without ceremony. "What was it?"

Ben took a breath and focused intently on the inside of his mug. He knew it was going to be hard, but he had seriously underestimated how much he didn't want to do this. He wished he hadn't given his word. "Mum told me some things while I was looking after her at the end; things that I don't remember her mentioning before. Like... she grew up here... in Farthing. She went to school here."

"Here? She grew up *here*? Really?" That blew his mind. "Which house was theirs?"

Their address was the least important detail to Ben, but then, he had to admit – he knew the rest of the story. "Perkins Road is named after their place. The family was well respected in this area."

To Liam, as he thought about it, this fitted what he knew. Of course, their name would be well regarded. Their mother had shared stories of being Elizabeth Perkins, the pampered daughter in a small rural community. But it was rather strange to realise it was this community. This isolated, country, dusty, little settlement just didn't seem like the setting for the pictures of the memories she had painted in their mind. In some ways it took away the mystique that had been created around her idyllic childhood. Liam never questioned the disparity of knowing his mother grew up as an indulged only child, and yet his grandparents were remote, austere people who had very little to do with them. He remembered visiting Grandmother during the Christmas holidays, and those stays were, without fail, an exercise in restraint that the twins were always glad to put behind them. They were never anticipated visits.

"After Mum left school she worked for the Stock and Station Agent in town here. His name was Madsen... that's a rather influential force in town. His son runs the agency now."

"Huh. I think I met him. The post-office was shut when we arrived, so I went there to get directions. The old guy doesn't like you much, does he?"

"You met Bill Madsen?"

"I wouldn't call it a meeting. He was scathing and uncouth. I didn't let on I wasn't you of course, and as far as I know he never twigged. Complimented you on the cut of my suit though. Felt like old times."

"Huh. Sounds like him. Who else did you meet?"

Now Ben admitted to himself he was avoiding the issue.

Liam grinned. "Felt like the whole town was at market that day. The common theme was relief you'd finally improved your wardrobe. And having another woman was something to talk about."

"There's a scandal that will outlive your visit. But then, controversy is not new to our family."

Liam looked at him and grinned. "Now I'm interested. I can't imagine Mum being controversial about anything. Although no surprise that Grandmother was antagonistic enough to cause waves."

Ben looked down at the ground. Would he say this? He poured out the dregs from his mug on the ground, took the billy off the fire, kicked dust over the ashes. He was stalling. Would this shatter the gold-plated picture of his mother? Would his brother still be able to love her, or himself, if he knew? He nearly didn't. Then he said, "If you choose to stay here in Farthing, it is only fair that you know that things happened while Mum was here. They are not all rose-coloured." He picked up another biscuit and choked on a crumb. He took a drink from his canvas water-bag as he sat down again. Liam noticed how uncomfortable Ben was and felt dread swell in the pit of his diaphragm. Ben swallowed again before continuing. "That bloke you met, Bill Madsen, he doesn't like me because I threatened to expose his secret."

"What secret?"

"That would be us."

"Us?"

"Mum got pregnant to him while she was working there. That Madsen is our biological father. William Benjamin Madsen. We are named after him... not just our grandparents on Dad's side."

Liam stared at him stunned. He paused and shook his head as if he didn't quite comprehend. For a moment Ben felt relieved. It was out, and he had over-estimated how hard Liam would take it. Ben looked at his brother and shrugged. Liam opened his mouth, but nothing came out. He slowly put down the mug in his hand; then barrelled Ben directly from where he was sitting and started punching into him like a madman. It took a moment for Ben, pinned to the ground in the dust to get his footing, but as soon as he did, he rolled over and returned the favour.

Ellen was sitting on the verandah showing Meg some finer mending techniques on some of Eliza's stockings, and she started to her feet in shock. She had never seen a street fight, and she had certainly never witnessed her husband behaving as if he was in a pub-brawl. She was mortified at this display of unprecedented violence and was shocked that her husband was in there doing his fair share. It stunned her senses as she watched dust fly and scaffolding tumble as they crashed and smashed around the worksite. Meg put down her knitting and reached out and placed a restraining hand on Ellen's arm. "You have to let them do this."

"No, I don't! They are hurting each other!"

"Yes. They do seem to be taking it quite seriously."

"We have to do something!"

"Come inside if you don't want to look."

"I can't just walk away and pretend they are still mixing up mortar. They are killing each other!"

"I doubt that. They need to work out how they can do this together."

"This is not the way! How can they work together if they are going to behave like street-dogs? This is dreadful! Meg, make them stop! You can't approve of this."

"This is not just stag-fighting on a hill Ellen. Ben's told him something that has really upset him."

"Well that is obvious. What could possibly be that bad?"

"We will probably find out soon enough."

"Why would Ben tell him something if he knew it would anger him so?"

"I guess he thought it was best."

"How is this best? This is dreadful! It is all Ben's doing."

"The way I saw it… Liam struck first."

"Then he must have been severely provoked. Everyone says they are alike, but Liam would never start something like this."

"Perhaps…" Meg shrugged and turned away. She didn't want to look either.

"Don't get all high mighty Meg. If Ben knew... he should have left it alone."

"So, if Liam ever tells you this provoking news and you don't like it... But maybe you're right; maybe he won't say. Maybe he'll leave it alone."

"Nothing he could possibly have to say would..." She straightened up and lifted her chin. "We have no secrets."

"Then I guess at some stage you will know what it's about." Meg looked back at them still crashing around the building site. Ben was certainly physically fitter of the two, but she could see even at this distance, his shoulder was causing a handicap. While that made the playing field more even, it prolonged the battle. Eventually they slowed. Even in their exhaustion, Liam still hit out, Ben blocking with his good arm.

Suddenly Ellen remembered the children. She called out to them and found them under the water tank, in full view of the shed site, and the brawl. Eliza was crying while her little brother was smugly standing back surveying the battle between his dad and uncle. Through her sobs Eliza showed some raised welts from Jensen's punches. Ellen smacked him soundly and then cringed at her own use of force. She sent him to sit on his swag, while she washed Eliza's tear-stained cheeks. The whole world was going mad!

Meg poured a couple of basins of water and got the

salve from the cupboard. Eventually they heard Ben's tread on the verandah. He came through the door like a foot solider returning from a war-front.

"What have you done? Why would you make him fight you so?" Ellen cried.

"He ain't fighting me," was all he said as Meg ushered him to a chair. He winced silently as she started to wash the cuts on his face.

Ellen turned around and slapped him hard across the face. He saw it coming but was too beat to bother blocking it. "That's ridiculous! You were going at it hammer and tong," she ranted, and stormed off outside.

Ben gave a tired shrug and sat while Meg started to wash his cuts. Ellen returned after a while. Ben was sitting still at the table, looking straight ahead.

"Where's is he? Why hasn't he come? How could you just leave him out there?"

"I'm reckoning he needs some time," he said.

"He is hurt. I need to tend him too," she blustered. Ellen went back to the verandah and stared out. She came back and sat down and then got up again to look through the window.

Ben leaned back in the chair, feeling the water washing over his skin, as Meg irrigated his cuts. How soothing her touch was, so different from the jerking, harsh treatments when she dressed his shoulder wound. "You're getting better at this," he said with a tired grin.

As she peeled back his shirt Ellen turned around and gasped as she saw his scars. "Oh, my goodness. What happened to you?"

Meg said nothing. Eventually Ben said, "Told you that story. I got shot."

Ellen stared at Meg like a monster had materialised out of the wood panelling in the living room. "You did that? I thought you were kidding! You people are crazy!"

Meg said nothing. Alistair's favourite by-line rang in her ear: "Every action has an equal and opposite reaction – a consequence". Newton's wisdom, so often quoted by Alistair, was less inspirational just now, and sounded more like the gavel of a judge. She found herself drawing on Ben's silence: strength to keep breathing. She became very aware that he, even battered and silent, was stabilising her. She continued to wash away the dust that had caked his skin. Twice she went out to retrieve a fresh pitcher of water and was sick as she leaned against the tank-stand. When she poured the water into the bowl on the table, she turned to Ellen, and said, "You might want to the take the kids out; I have to look at the cut on his leg now." Ellen hustled them away through the door, grabbing the bran-cake from the bench on the way out.

Ben stood up and took off his torn trousers. Blood had soaked through a makeshift bandage he had wrapped around it and he propped his leg up on a chair. Meg gagged and dry retched. She had nothing left, but felt clammy and sat down heavily for a moment to catch her breath. When she stood up, Ben looked at her apologetically. "Think we're going to have to stitch this."

"I'm not doing that. I'll take you to Doctor Mansfield."

"I ain't driving ten miles into town for a scratch."

"It's not a scratch, or it wouldn't need stitching."

"I need you to do this; I can't reach it from here to do a good job on it."

She closed her eyes and swallowed. "Ellen is not any help; she is absolutely out of her mind. Okay. Let's do this." She braced herself; went and got her sewing kit and a candle. She burnt the needles like Doctor Mansfield had shown her. Again, she swabbed the wound, and slowly joined the sides. Ben reassured her it didn't have to be pretty, but it had to be strong. As the last stitch was tied off, she went as white as a sheet and came too propped up on pillows on her bed, with Ben fanning her face and wiping her forehead with a damp cloth.

Meg looked up. The welts on Ben's face were starting to show purple, his lip was split, and dried blood was speared over his chin where he had wiped at it. "I'm guessing Liam wasn't all that comfortable with what you told him," she said faintly.

"It took me six months solid, and three years all up to get used to it. He's not going to get his head around it in an hour and a half." Ben handed her some sweet tea, and she sipped it.

"Guess this means they won't stay," she offered.

"We'll see…"

Liam didn't come in that night until after supper. He didn't eat. He just grabbed a drink from the water jug and went straight to bed. Ellen stared in horror at the dried blood and the purple swelling around his eye. She tearfully objected to him lying on the linen in his filthy clothes, but Meg gently touched her arm, and offered to help wash in the morning. Then she went and got ready for bed to allow them at least some symbolic sense of privacy. Sometime during the night, she stirred as Ben got up and followed Liam out onto the verandah. He sat down on the stair.

"You've got no proof. That was just the delirious ravings of a dying woman," Liam said sullenly, slumped on the settee.

"Never seen her more lucid," said Ben looking at the stars.

"There is no proof," he insisted.

"She gave me a letter Madsen wrote her. After she told him, he tried to convince her to get rid of 'the problem'. He was willing to pay. When he refused to marry her, she told her family, and they left town. It would have been unbearable had it got out."

"Why couldn't she just let it be? She held it in for twenty-five years. She didn't have to say anything."

"She had nothing to gain by telling this story. She wanted us to know the truth but didn't know how to tell you."

"This is ridiculous. Did Dad even know?"

"Yeah. He married her knowing full well that she may never love him. Their age difference caused a stir, but Mum said she saw it as a lifeline. It was her chance of survival. Dad's standing in the community provided a way for her to keep her family's reputation intact, and that's why they allowed it. He never told anyone that we were not his. They didn't know she was expecting twins until the birth, but that worked for them and made the early dates seem reasonable."

"I feel like I can't see anymore. It changes every single thing! Was everything about our life a lie? I never knew she didn't love him."

"She did though. Every time she told us she was proud of us, had a wonderful husband and a blessed life... she meant it. She wasn't just saying it."

"Kinda explains why we don't have the Harker nose. Everyone used to say I was like Dad and your personality more like Mum."

"Not everything is about blood. He was still our father: Of course the person he was, would rub off on us."

Liam just shook his head and blew his nose. "All

mum's piety. And all along she was an adulterous whore.
We are just bastards!"

"But we aren't illegitimate: Dad gave us his name. We
were born as *his* sons into *his* household. Never did get why
he harped on that so much until mum told me this. Guess
he knew we might find out one day, and didn't want to be
displaced by a worthless teenage fling who couldn't stand up
and do the right thing."

"Is this why Susanna never liked Mum?"

"As far as I can tell both Susanna and Eunice don't
know. When you think about it, they were not much
younger than Mum when they married. They were still
reeling from their mother's accident and hated the idea that
Dad caved so quickly after her funeral to marry someone
else. Nothing was said about the pregnancy until after the
honeymoon.   They   just   saw   the   betrayal   of   an
inappropriately quick romance and a gold digger."

"Well she was."

"She was a lonely, scared teenager in a strange
community who was dumped by her boyfriend, and her
family was disowning her. She had nothing… except this
one kindness. It was her sacrifice too, to keep us. She said
she never, ever regretted that."

"How can you be so cool about it? This is outrageous!
Everything I thought I was is a lie!"

"You forget. I've been working through this for three
years. Every single thing you've said, I've said to myself.

Your own answers will come."

"Madsen. What's he like?"

"That's what I came to Farthing to find out. You met him. What you saw sounds pretty accurate."

"I feel sick. Didn't like him. At all."

"Me neither. He's a bastard... even if we are not."

"Are we contaminated? Hell. I don't know what to think! Is there any hope, knowing this is who we are?"

"I'm not taking him on. Jensen Harker is still my father. My only father. Madsen ain't my heritage. He ain't that good. Not even close."

"Doesn't change the facts. Does he know?"

"He does now. Told him the day we got married. We needed a loan. The man's as tight as a sea clam out of water. No way he would've given us anything without that sort of leverage."

"You could've asked me. We would have sorted something."

"It happened pretty quick. Meg wasn't going to marry me. When she changed her mind, I didn't want to wait."

"So, a loan... that's the business he spoke of. You're a sly one little brother." To Ben it sounded like a compliment: the first one in a long time.

"I don't trust Madsen as far as I can spit. I need to sell the furniture to pay him out. Was going to ask you to take it back and sell it – would get more than trying to do it here. Meg's selected out what she's going to keep."

Liam rubbed his puffy eye, the bruising coming up around the lid. "You seem so damn okay with this. How? I don't know how!"

He didn't say anything for a while. "I've had more time to work at it, I guess. And Meg... she gave me a chance even though she knew nothing about me, except that I was a cattle thief and that I tried to put her out of business."

"Grief Ben, you really did that? What the hell were you thinking? That's a low blow. Not to mention you could've got killed. My brother has fallen from a very high tree."

"I ain't proud. Just saying that's what happened. But when I went back to the simple decency I grew up with, Meg responded to that. I saw scum like our neighbour, and Madsen, with their fine horses and their flashy money pins, I realised my anger was feeding the part of me that was exactly what I didn't like in them. I didn't have to throw away the values we grew up with. That was my choice. I didn't understand the decision Mum was faced with until I came here. Meg is to me, what Dad was for Mum. Just like Mum said: those who are forgiven much, love much. I've had to search that truth for myself."

"Good for you... but I didn't screw up. I'm just living my life and suddenly someone tips me down the long-drop."

"What I realised is that God always knew who I am and he loves me anyway. That is true as much now, as when I didn't know all this about myself. That's never changed.

The only thing that has changed is my awareness of it."

"I thought it was me who wanted to be a preacher. Guess that's off the table now."

"If you're called, you're still called. I ain't called that's all."

"Huh. I don't even know if I was. Perhaps I just thought I was good enough to do it... and now I'm not."

"Liam... you'll find your way through this. I know that."

"I need to see that letter."

"It's in the safety deposit box back home, where I had the ring."

"What? It was just there... among those papers? I wish sometimes I were more nosey. Well, then... I'm going to get it. I need to see it."

"Fair enough. You gotta do what you gotta do. But you ain't doing that alone."

They sat on the verandah and watched the sun rise. It seemed bizarre to Liam that the sun still came up in the east like nothing monumental had been uncovered. Just another day. Ellen came out in the morning and saw them sitting there. She had cried herself to sleep, confused and displaced by this sudden, inexplicable change in her respectable Liam. It felt like her eyes were unveiled and the simple, clean living of country life was being exposed as a villain in ragged clothes. Where was the wholesome community that yesterday was perceived as close and supportive? Now it seemed gossipy and fraught with danger? What else did they know that she didn't?

As she returned from the out-house, Liam stood to his feet. "Walk with me Ellen. I've got something to tell you."

Candid fear washed over her face. A walk. A talk. She was being summoned to court to be told a verdict that had already been handed down with no right of reply. They walked for a while. "I'm going back home with Ben – to sell Mum's furniture. He needs the money to pay out a loan. I want you to stay with Meg while we are gone. When I come back, we will decide whether we stay and work the quarry, or whether we just leave things the way they are."

Ellen looked sideways at her husband. She felt fear strangling her throat with the threat that nothing would ever be the same. "Liam, what's this about? What did Ben say to you?"

"Just some family stuff. We'll be back soon enough. It shouldn't take long."

"Why won't you tell me? I am your wife! I have a right to know!"

"It's just something I need to do. And I need Ben there to help with the sale otherwise I'd go by myself. You'll be okay here I'm sure. You said you wanted to stay on with

Meg for a bit. Now's your chance."

"But not like this. Are you leaving me?"

"What?"

"Are you having some sort of breakdown and leaving us?"

He shook his head sort of dazed. He really didn't need this just now. "I think... never mind. We'll be back next week."

Ellen burst into tears. She had defended their relationship... their lack of secrets... their togetherness. What a joke! Laughable that he would stand there and say it was something he needed to do. She needed her husband to tell her what was going on. That's what she needed! He reached out awkwardly to touch her arm and she shook him off like some sort of spider, turned around and walked back to the house.

Liam stared after her retreating figure. Even Ellen could feel the contamination. She wanted nothing to do with him. He flew at the tree standing by the track, kicking the butt of its trunk in a rage.

Ellen grabbed the basket off the bench and collected the eggs so she could start breakfast. Everything was all out of kilter and it was scaring her.

Meg came out as Ellen was setting the table. Meg looked at her face and said, "What's happened? Did he tell you?"

"No, he didn't. They are going back home to sell the

furniture. That's what he says, but it can't be just that. He won't say!" Her distress was pulling at her face in all sorts of angles. She sat down hard. "Meg, I think there is another woman. Perhaps that is what Ben said to him... confronted his behaviour. Maybe that is why he won't leave the city... because there is someone else."

Meg looked at her sitting there bent and broken. It was so unfair that she knew and Ellen didn't. "I don't think he would take his brother to meet his mistress. Ellen, that is someone you hide away, not introduce to your family. I'm pretty confident you are his only love."

Ellen scoffed. "Love?" Tears rolled down her face. She was being irrational, but the fear was crushing her. There is nothing rational about being terrified and confused; confronted by a stranger in your bed. Meg poured her a cup of tea and wordlessly pushed it towards her. Ellen gulped it. It scalded her throat and somehow that felt comforting.

"Ellen, you said before that you and Liam have no secrets. Surely if that is so, this will be no different. Can't it be, that perhaps going away will help him talk about it when he gets back? This has obviously thrown him."

"You know what this is about, don't you?"

Meg looked at her. How she wanted to lie outright. "Ben hasn't said what he talked to Liam about... exactly... but I, you are right: I do know. It is why Ben came to Farthing after his mother died. He needed to sort it through then. Liam is going to need some space to do that now."

"Why does he get to do that, when it leaves me out in the dark? Tell me what it is."

"Ellen, you know that is not my place."

"No one seems to appreciate that it is my place to know what my husband is going through!"

Meg went and gave her a hug. Nausea and reflux burned her throat and she quickly went outside. She realised then the waves of sickness were less severe and not as often, more like a background wash of unsettling green. At least she could stand upright. She refused to think about Ben going away in case she started to submit to the horror of the last time she was pregnant, and her husband left... forever. The distraction of Ellen's distress was keeping her afloat.

Ben and Liam restacked the wagon and tarped it up. Ben stretched the sisal rope tightly and tied it down. "How did Ellen take it?"

Liam said nothing while he anchored another knot. It was pretty obvious: she wasn't taking anything well at the moment. "I didn't tell her. Just said we are going to sell the furniture."

"So, she doesn't know what's going on?"

"I'm not going to tell her something that I don't even know for sure is true. I'll work it out when we get back."

Ben bit the reproach that was sitting on his tongue. After his mother had dropped this particular load on him, he wished someone, anyone, had not been uncomfortable with his confusion. How he had wanted someone not to expect his horror to go away, or be explained, or want him to be reasonable. He resolved to be that person he never had. He went to Meg and took her by the hand and led her outside. "You know I wish I could be in two places at once."

"I don't want you to go..."

"You've done alone for so long it seems unfair that you have to do it again. I've organised for one of the boys from the quarry to come and do the chores, and the crew will bring more stone down so that it's ready for when we get back. You can talk to the foreman if you're worried about anything. Frank's a good bloke."

"Ellen is here, and the distraction is helping. Liam didn't tell her."

"I know." He didn't really know what else to say.

"I'm trying so hard not to put my foot in it, but she is struggling Ben. Can't you convince him to at least give her something?"

He shook his head.

"Nothing? That is so unfair."

"I'm glad you are with her though. Will help keep her grounded."

"Really? Grounded? Her whole world is falling apart, and you think it is my job to keep her feet on the ground?"

"Well you know what it's like... not knowing. I reckon it is one of the hardest places to be. You might be able to help her."

"She's imagining all sorts of horrors. I can't tell her anything. Liam refuses to. Exactly how do you think I am going to help?"

"Meg, I can't force him to tell her. This is his stuff to share with her."

"Just get back as soon as you can then. It will be nothing short of horrific."

They drove off early the next morning before the sun had risen. The dew from the night beading over the tarp covered wagon as they disappeared behind the bank of trees lining the track, shrouded in the grey pre-dawn light.

15.

They sat in a small room where a smoky overhead lamp cast an eerie shadow across their task. Ben turned the key and opened the metal lid to the security box. He rifled through the documents and pulled out a small yellowed, water-stained envelope addressed simply to "Betty". He paused and handed it to his brother. Liam recoiled as if being asked to handle an apple encircled by a snake: the very thing he wanted could well be the death of him. Ben paused then and put it on the table in front of him.

Liam stared at it. Eventually he took a breath and unfolded its contents. He read through dry eyes, an angry flush running along his temples. The writing was formal and cold in its immaturity: a boy trying to sound more man than he was. Perhaps Madsen thought the stilted language would add weight to his position, justifying cowardice. Liam could not believe that this was addressing his mother. Much easier to think he was reading some poorly written, sordid novel. But what the letter did, was add weight to that big question: was this real? He wished now he could storm into the kitchen and demand answers of his mother, spooning biscuit mixture onto a baking tray and humming a tune on her lips. How dare she be content! How dare she hold this shame over his father! How dare she be something other than what he always thought!

He put it back on the table. Ben took it, folded it up and put it back in the box. "Why do you keep it?" Liam rasped.

"The same reason Mum did. It is the only thing we have that says it was real. Without it, I would not have believed her perhaps. Ironically, the fact he tried to keep the tone of the letter official and distant means all the details needed to prove who it refers to are in there. Then he signed it. Stupid really."

"How can life ever be the same?"

"It won't be the same... at least for me. This has changed me. But it doesn't have to be for the worse."

"Damn! How can she dump this on us and then just die; leave us to pick up the pieces. Why didn't she say something before?"

"She'd made her peace with it, I guess. I have too. Now it is your turn."

"I can't! I just can't! It is extraordinary that you expect me too!"

Ben looked down at his work-roughened hands. Liam used to mock those hands, because they were more comfortable on a building site than with the prestige of directing a project through the design. The very idea of being a labourer was distasteful to Liam. For Ben, hands-on was simply more interesting. That was all. And just for a moment, Ben wondered if arrogance was genetic like Madsen strutting around in his suit. And then he checked himself, and acknowledged such thinking had its own brand of toffiness that wasn't just about flash clothes.

They went outside in the sunlight, and the glare seemed to expose their secret to the world. Liam pulled his hat down hard over his eyes. Ben adjusted his brim with a tilt. They had a meeting with an auctioneer, and then afterwards they sat at the Café on Lane, staring down the busy street while they waited for their orders to be taken. Commuters were coming and going; men in suits, women with perambulators, ladies with parasols.

Liam sort of groaned. "Life goes on. My world has been ripped apart and no one gives a toss."

"This is true."

"But I want them to notice. I want them to know life is changed!"

"Or perhaps you want to pretend it never happened."

"When did you become such an insolent know-it-all? But you might be right. It's safer this doesn't get out. After all – that's why they left Farthing."

"Liam? Ben? Oh, my goodness, look at you two!"

Ben stood to his feet. "Eunie? Sis, you are still here?" He enveloped her in a hug.

"Of course. I promised Elizabeth it would stay in our family: Café on Lane is truly a Harker venture. It has the taste of home. It is where I learnt that cooking is made of smiles. Oh, it is good to see you two ragamuffins! Breakfast on the house. Johns – keep their coffee cups full!" She pulled a chair over and sat down.

Ben grinned at her enthusiasm. The quiet Eunice had found her voice. "You look well. How's Susanna?"

"Oh, you know. Busy... she is like the conductor of her own personal orchestra... keeps everything in time and in tune around her. She doesn't come here often. She never really got on board with the controversy of Dad buying a business for Elizabeth. It is still her opinion that is unseemly for a proper lady to be working. Jonathan and Joseph are both studying now... law. And little Susan is no longer little. Debutante this year... and she has a line of suitors trying to find their way around her mother."

"And you...?"

"Oh, you know. I have my little café... and..." She blushed. "...an interested gentleman. I am doing okay. It has been hard though without Elizabeth to go to. Your mother was very generous to me..."

"Mum would like it that the café continues on in safe Harker hands. She always said you were the only one who appreciated it in all its 'gory and glory'."

"Well sometimes I think it is like a child... messy and has its tantrums; busy times and lazy times... and then I try to whip it into shape. But this is my life and I can't imagine anything else."

"The interested guy... is he good to you?"

"He is." And she nodded and introduced them to Johns as he filled their coffee cups again and did the rounds of other customers. "We work well together. I never thought after Phillip passed, that I would find someone else. Come and see me before you go and we will make a time to have dinner together. I want to hear about you." She stood up apologetically. "I have to go… but dinner. Don't forget. I'll make Pot Roast and your Mum's apple-cake."

Liam stared at Eunice attending to the customers at a far table. "I can't go to dinner and play happy family! Not happening. Not even for apple-cake."

"I'm not going to tell her. Still she is family. This family is what Dad and Mum fought for. She doesn't need to know anything more that. What they chose to tell her is enough. But I needed Meg at least had to know the truth about me. And you. We all need someone who knows us…"

Liam grunted and stared at his coffee. "Can't think why that would be a good idea. This is not worth knowing."

"How are you going to tell Ellen?"

"I have no idea. You know her family Ben. If she ever let it slip, they would never let it go. She has grown up with every sort of privilege. We used to talk about how fortunate it was that we were so alike. That freaks me out. We were matched. And now we are not."

"There must be something in Farthing that Ellen feels it can offer. Big move to make if everything is better at home."

"What are you saying?"

"You tell me. Why does she want to move?"

"Well, I don't know.　She just gets these ideas sometimes."

"So, you've never asked her."

"Well, doesn't that sound like you've got it all figured out!　I recall Meg having a go at her husband because she knew squat about your background."　He went quiet as Johns put down his plate and he tackled his serve of fried eggs, bacon, and toast with force.　"It's a small hut," Liam observed through a mouthful of food as he sprinkled more salt on his meal.

"I ain't saying I've got it sorted: I'm just saying.　I'm working this out too.　I don't know how to do this married thing, but I've spent a lot of time thinking, about you and Ellen, Dad and Mum.　I have admired your relationship with Ellen: she's pretty; smart; stoic as hell.　It gave me hope that Meg might give me a chance.　The thing I didn't expect was... the idea of letting Meg know all of me... the truth about me... the ugly stuff, as well as the good.　Meg saw a lot of ugly.　She copped that and loved me anyway.　But then I got all embarrassed about the good.　But that isn't fair.　Maybe it's the other way around for you.　Time for ugly."

"I don't do ugly."

"You've been married for six years.　No man alive can keep up a charade of no ugly in that time.　Don't care how well they dress."

"This is not helping Ben!　You're supposed to be helping me figure this out.　What if she can't do it?　I can't lose her."

Ben looked at his brother and realised the fear was real. "Dunno. A skeleton or two takes some getting used to. But I'm thinking that woman would follow you to Africa if she thought that was what you wanted."

"Huh. Africa might be an option."

"She belted me after we had that fight you know."

"She hit you?" He grinned with an unexpected feeling of satisfaction.

"She is loyal Liam, and I'm thinking is it is not just this sanitised idea that you have of yourself. She loves you man. Ugly bits and all."

Ben salted his sausages and ate without saying anything for a while. Johns topped up their coffee again. A passer-by paused and looked them over. "Well! The Harker Boys are back in town! Just like old times, scratched up and bruised, still looking like you own the joint. How long you back for?"

Ben shrugged non-committedly. Liam put down his coffee and smiled amiably. "Ellen's staying with Ben's wife out in the country for a bit while we tie up some things from the estate."

"Married hey Ben? I know some ladies around here who will be disappointed about that." Ben shrugged vaguely into his coffee.

Liam diverted their talk to their pending move to Farthing. "All but a done deal," he concluded with a nod.

"Well, good for you. Now don't be a stranger." And he left without any further pause.

Ben raised his eyebrows and shrugged. "Who?"

Liam looked at his retreating figure, pleased that he was recognised. "Some guy."

"You don't know?"

"Not a clue..." and he grinned because he had pulled off the conversation without giving himself away.

"Come on Liam – this is exactly what I was talking about. Why tell a stranger stuff you won't talk to Ellen about?"

"Was just making conversation. It means nothing. The guy doesn't even know us."

"Well enough to know we'd been away... and we are back."

"Just trying to get my head around it – that's all."

"Huh." He said nothing for a long time. Eventually Ben drained his cup and said, "I wonder if that's why Mum told... because she wanted us to know more than just the presentable side. That's encouraged me – knowing failure was retrievable. I think she wanted us to know that is possible. That means a lot, given how monumentally I have stuffed up."

"Well I liked having parents who didn't have skeletons. Up to now, the most controversial thing in my life was their age difference. Hell, that is so insignificant now; it means nothing... and I used to think that was so

155

sickening."

"What Dad did, what he knew... yet he kept it just between them. I'm..." Ben let out a sigh. "I dunno... I just feel that he was never given the credit he deserved for being the man that he was. This was his way of fighting to protect us... and mostly he just got flack for being a cradle snatcher. It injured his reputation, yet he never caved. He took it to his grave. I wish I could let him know... that I get it... and that I respect him for it. Don't know that he knew that."

Liam signalled for a refill of coffee. He put his elbows on the table and rubbed his forehead... a social faux pas that his mother would never have tolerated. He suddenly looked up. "What do you mean it injured his reputation?"

"Mum said that the firm... after they married, the partners became very obstructive... something about his first wife's family. They couldn't push him out completely because he was a founding partner and held a dominant share, but they tried. So, he went into a type of silent partnership..."

"But he used to say that he did that because it gave him more flexibility to spend time with us boys."

"Wasn't his first choice apparently. They came up with an agreement that excluded him from having private clients, so he did other jobs... book-keeping and such... but architecture... that was his first love. Mum said that was the first time they disagreed – she tried to convince him to disclose why they married so the firm would see his virtue and take him back, but he absolutely refused. Said it wouldn't go down that way. By stepping aside, he negotiated to leave the door open for us to have an internship if we wanted it. That's why he would always take us into town on Fridays. Remember how we'd have lunch in the park looking at buildings and talk about architecture. He wanted to keep the dream alive. You have his shares Liam, because he fought for them."

Liam grunted and drained his coffee. "And I thought it was because I didn't want all the household paraphernalia you got landed with. This debacle touches everything... even the firm is contaminated. Guess that makes sense though, why I am kept in the back room like some shameful leper. They said it was my age: that I had to put in the time. But Dad was right – they could never have known. I've always wanted to be included in that men's club, but now leaving would be no sacrifice at all."

"Really? We get to do the quarry?" He felt relief, even excitement, rising.

"Huh. Now you're on board. I don't know that Farthing is the only alternative to leaving the firm. Like you said: there is always Africa. How can you stand being in a place where no one knows the truth about anything? Here they think Dad's the villain; they think the firm has professional integrity; there Madsen's the player. It's all a lie."

"Oh, people know Madsen. But regardless, I'm not there for him. Meg wants to stay, so I stay. What she knows is more important than what anyone else thinks. That is the choice Dad made. Mum knew and that was enough. It sits well with me to follow that line."

"Noble, no doubt. Think you might have wrecked it though. You told Madsen."

"He already knew his part in this remember... and he's not going to tell anyone about his shame. Jolly sure the truth is secure there. Look, I know you think it's risky telling Ellen. But not telling her will create a different set of problems."

"Not telling her is the way I can protect her, like Dad's silence."

"But Dad never included Mum in the silence."

Liam stood to his feet and slapped his brother on the shoulder... his bad shoulder – deliberately of course. "Ben you're a naggin' old hag. You're going to have to quit on that, because we're going home tomorrow and I'm not gunna listen to your whinging all the way back."

16.

Meg sat in the shade with her back against the cool stone wall as a backdrop to their lunch. Meg resented that her pregnancy had catapulted her into a confinement where she couldn't do farm work or help with the construction. Liam and Ellen had driven off in the cart with Jensen waving his shanghai frantically, and Eliza clutching her little knitted doll like a life buoy. Since they left Meg firmly insisted on this lunchtime ritual as a way of proving she was not a mother who needed wrapping in cotton wool. Ben had taken on one of the young guys from the quarry crew who knew stone, so the progress continued on the building almost without pause.

She noticed changes though. Since coming back Ben seemed stronger, more available, more tender. Her heart swelled as she was bathed in a grateful sense of confidence in the future: their future. It was like that once dark marital room was being opened up: the curtains pulled back; the rugs spring-cleaned; the furniture polished. It was a room that was becoming familiar and comfortable. There were things more frightening than delivery. She had done that. In all of its horror she had survived. But being alone... again... doing that... *that* was more than she could contemplate. That she would fight. And as she sat on a cushion positioned strategically on a block of masonry in the shade of the stone wall, she worked her way through the weeks, and her fears.

She shifted her weight again, stiff and uncomfortable, pushing the baby across as it moved under her diaphragm. She wondered if this bloated state would petrify her body in the stone they were working with. She leant over and picked up a slab of corn meat and folded it between bread that had been smeared with dripping. Ben hooked the billy off the little fire with a poker and poured a couple of drinks. He took the bread from her hand, and a kiss from her lips. "I can do that. You don't have to," he murmured.

She raised her eyebrow in a challenge. "I'm not an invalid you know."

"Ain't game enough to be accusing you of that." He paused and looked at her. "You know Doc Mansfield agrees we should not stay out here. You are past the date he gave to go in, and after last time Meg I really want you in town… near help."

"Humph. It's ridiculous." She straightened her back and shifted her weight. "I do it alone with no one around and it doesn't turn a head. This time I have people fawning over me like I'm completely incapable of doing very basic woman's work."

"It's just a precaution. If we lived closer to town, I'd be none too worried."

"I can remember you telling me that you would be embarrassed to go to town for a 'scratch'. Well, birthing is a normal part of life… and less intrusive than having a leg so slashed up that it required eighteen stitches."

"Meg I will hog-tie you and take you in, if I have to. I'm not going to be responsible for things going wrong."

"Why do you always assume the worst? Doc Mansfield says I'm very healthy."

"I'm not assuming the worst. I just couldn't handle it, if it did go wrong. There are already too many people mustered up there in that picket fence on the hill. Not my daughter, Meg. Nor you." He wondered if he could scare her into complying.

That made her smile. "So, you think you are getting a girl? Why is that so?"

"Because I can't imagine our family without a girl that takes after her mother. She would be perfect. Stubborn as hell… but perfectly beautiful."

"And if it's a boy?"

"Well, probably won't be as pretty… but he'll be able to shoot just as fine I'm sure." He came and knelt beside her. "Please… don't be resisting me on this. I'm not one to pull rank, but on this I really want to insist."

She looked at him and the set of her jaw softened. She kissed his forehead. "I just had this picture of starting our family… out here together. Not in mourning… not alone. Just us. If we go in there the midwife won't allow you near me, and I won't see you for days. I want to share this with you. Please."

He shook his head amazed. "Damned if I know how you can be so calm about this! Why aren't you worried?"

"Who says I am not? Ben, not having you with me… unorthodox as that is… that scares me."

"Yet you seem calm. You aren't pacing or talking nonsense."

"I never talk nonsense. And even if I was inclined: moving is too uncomfortable just now to pace. Besides, you are here."

"That's ridiculous. I don't have a clue. And I'm terrified."

"Relax…" and she grimaced and stood up to stretch, rubbing the low ache in her back. Actually, everything ached. "Take a leaf out of the baby's book. It seems she likes to spread out… so I'm thinking she's going to be a relaxed sort of child."

The way she explained the reasons behind her stubborn snub of Doc Mansfield's recommendations touched the core of his soul. How could he challenge that? He got up and strode around the building site. The irony that he was pacing in lieu of her calm was not lost on him. And yet, he had to be prepared. He had to have a plan. He had taken a short-term lease on a vacant house in town, but Meg refused to go. That was not a plan; that was obstinate! As natural and normal as childbirth was, people died from doing it. That was a reality that scared the hell out of him.

17.

After dinner Meg sat with her feet up. She had eaten very little and her ankles were swollen. It seemed her whole body was groaning in anticipation of delivering this precious life to her parents. "Ben?"

"Hmm?"

"Are you disappointed that Liam decided not to stay? You haven't said much about it since they went."

"Yes and no. I didn't realise how much I missed him 'til he was here: strutting his stuff, arguing his point, and doing the family thing. That's how we always were. And I liked that you hit it off so well with Ellen. I thought it was good you had some womanly company. So maybe disappointed. But it had to be right for them... and it wasn't... so what can I do?"

"I was surprised Ellen was so angry when Liam told her. I really thought she'd be relieved. She was frantic over the idea he was being unfaithful. Even before you left, she told me she didn't believe the furniture was anything more than a ruse to introduce you to his mistress."

"That would take some serious impertinence. She was right though... it was a front. I didn't want him reading that letter by himself."

"I still don't understand why the whole thing evaporated. Ellen said the 'being-conceived-out-ofwedlock' shame didn't matter half as much to her as it did to him. If it didn't matter, why not move out here like they planned?" She had lost her only chance to be family, in the extended way of being family. Meg shifted position again. Her back was really aching. She didn't really know why she brought it up just now; they had been gone for months. She wistfully thought what it would mean to have Ellen with her just now. She stopped then, as if something dawned on her. Echoes of another day, lying on her bed mourning Alistair, her body responding to the spasms of her broken heart with its own version of agony. So, she had thought.

Ben shrugged and considered his drink. He wasn't so much interested in the process as the bottom line. When they couldn't settle on moving to Farthing, they maintained the status quo. That's what he had to deal with. He decided he would propose a partnership with Liam anyway, even remotely. The more he thought about it, he liked the reassurance of being able to access his brother's business creativity which such a partnership would offer. He had savvy and smarts. Liam had vision and drive. It was a balance he wanted to capitalise on. All that was true, but he recognised Meg was detouring him from the issue at hand.

"Meg? What if we go and stay at the house… in town, just until the baby is born? That way we can do it like you said… just us, starting our family together. But then if we need to call the midwife, we can do it without delay. Like a back-up plan," he qualified quickly.

"Benjamin Harker, you are not going to give up, are you? I really think you would go to hog-tying. Do I have no choice in this at all?"

He raised his glass and smiled knowingly. Finally, she was relenting. That was easier than he thought it would be. He expected another couple of days of fortifying herself behind battlements at least.

"Then I'm thinking we should go tonight," she said with a dismissive shrug.

"Sure..." he said as he calmly sipped his drink. "That's a great plan. Driving into town in the dark, hitting every rock and ditch because we can't see. That'd put you into solid labour for certain."

"Well don't accuse me of not telling you then," she said lightly and picked up a book to read. The pages were left unturned.

"What do you mean?" He looked at her keenly. "Meg?"

She said nothing but stared at her book, focussing hard on the print.

"Meg? Damn it! How long have you known? Were you deliberately hiding this from me?"

"Ben, it's labour. It's one of those things that can't be hidden. If I was in labour, I guarantee you would know about it."

"Then what? Why would you want to go tonight? Are you serious?"

"Ben I've told you: I don't want to go at all. But well, I'm thinking that if you are so set on this plan... then tomorrow... might be too late."

"Meg?" His tone was confounded.

"I don't know for sure. I've just have been aching all day. My back is killing me. I'm just wondering... if it is, well, you know... the start."

Ben knocked his drink and started to his feet. For a moment he felt completely disorientated. "But isn't it too early? Doc said we had a couple more weeks. There was supposed to be heaps of time! Hell... what do we do now? Do we go? Or not? Is it safe?"

Meg smiled, and then her face twisted a little to the side as she paused to catch her breath. "You said you've got the house sorted... so why don't we just make our way there. I don't think I'm going to sleep anyway for a while. There's no need to panic. By morning we will have a better idea if it is, or whether it's just one of those false starts."

Looking back, Ben said that night was one of the longest of his life. Meg might have seemed calm as Ben stowed their travel trunk and lifted the glass to light the lantern on each side of the buggy. He helped her up and flicked the reigns and they slowly started to make their way into town. The air was cool, but Ben pulled at his collar, hot and sweaty as he tried to swallow that awful taste of apprehension in his throat. Meg's stoically said nothing as they rolled and jolted, her cramping becoming more intense. It wasn't long before there were regular strong contractions that were taking her breath away.

As he came to each creek crossing Ben would get down and lead the horse across so that he wouldn't be spooked by the shadows, talking to them calmly in a monotone prattle. Soothing them had the effect of calming himself, and he would jump back up beside Meg a little more composed.

"I don't suppose you could talk to me like that. It's reassuring."

"Ain't saying anything sensible... just keeping them calm."

"That's what I need just now."

"Really? My horse? Meg you are not my horse." He said it as another contraction gripped, and she grabbed his forearm like a vice. As it eased, she didn't release the pressure and he looked at her sideways. "Meg?"

"Don't you be telling me just now that your horse is going to get more of your attention than your wife. It is a simple enough request. Just do it."

"But..."

"Ben! We have only just turned off Rocky Gully Road... so we are not even close to halfway. I'm not going to do this in silence so start your horse whispering or whatever you do, or else I'll be yelling and spooking your blessed horse wild."

Ben cleared his throat awkwardly and started quietly murmuring reassurances. He could feel Meg relax between each vice-like grip soothing her with his whispers.

It took them hours rattling across those dark roads, lit only by the light of a half moon and the flickering of their faded lanterns. When they pulled up in front of the house Ben jumped down and unlocked the front door, lighting the lamps inside. Meg scrambled down with Ben's hand and her footing slipped on the buggy step. She fell heavily against him, staying there as another contraction paralysed her.

"Meg? I'm thinking I'll get the doctor or the midwife… to let them know we are here."

"Just settle me in first," she said as she stood upright and brushed the damp hair back off her forehead. She stopped at the front step and leant over, a groan escaping.

He followed her inside. "Meg… please just let me get Doctor Mansfield."

Another contraction. When she stood up, he edged towards the door; she glared him down. "Ben Harker! Don't you dare be going! This predicament is as much your doing as mine, so you are not leaving me to it."

"He needs to know you are here."

"Rubbish. The man needs his sleep if there…" She stopped and stared at the mantle clock as she heard the strike of the hour, cringing as she counted through contractions. Three o'clock. She remembered what that was. Once with Alistair, and again lying alone on her bed holding the twisted body of her premature baby wrapped in a blanket. Three o'clock in the morning was a familiar horror. Three o'clock in the morning was the hour of death, not life.

Ben looked at her bewildered. Was she going to hold him hostage so that she would make staying at the farm seem like the more sensible option? He went to defend his case yet again, but there was a set about her jawline and her brow was puckered in unnatural creases.

"Fine. After daylight," she relented. "But not before. You are not leaving me alone, in the dark, in a run-down house that is not my own. Not caring for that."

18.

Meg laboured bravely all day and into the night again. She fluctuated through anxiety; and panic; fighting the fear and frustration and pain. Doc Mansfield came and went, and when the midwife came she cowered under Meg's strict concessions for her even being there. Ben paced back and forth. Would this end with Meg reliving the tragedy of another deformed baby with multiple life-threatening problems, who would end up resting with the others in the Petrea Downs graveyard? Ben stood at the window and watched the silver light of the moon quietly rest on the street before them, the same moon that fell across the undulating paddocks of Petrea Downs. The grave plot on the hill was now tended and tidy and peaceful. He swallowed his fear. Surely Meg would not join them too? Zinnias grew along the border of the white pickets; a red dog-rose bush growing beside the gravestone of Alistair, and a white one beside the matching headstone of their baby son: Alistair David McGregor, with a birth date, and just three words, "Faith, Hope, Love".

Meg resolutely calmed, and worked through her exhaustion with each contraction, pushing down hard, her hair wet on her forehead. Ben lifted his face from his folded arms, creased from the weight of sleep. He heard a cry and looked across the room to the bed where Meg lay and the midwife wrapped the slippery bundle, and then tied the cord and snipped him free, marking him for independent life. She wiped his eyes with a soft cloth, vernix thick around his scalp. It took Ben's breath away. A boy. The midwife checked him over. He was perfect. Ben reached out and took his son in his arms. He screwed up his little face and bellowed his welcome to the world.

"Jamin Alistair Harker, I baptise you in the name of the Father and of the Son and of the Holy Spirit." His face puckered and he let out a most unholy squawk. The congregation tittered and nodded and jabbed each other and prophesied that his parents would have their hands full with this one who was so willing to speak his mind when only a little more than a week old.

The minister stood with the parents at the door as everyone left the church and offered their blessings and congratulations. People tucked gifts of booties, baby blankets, bonnets, and soft toys into Jamin's carry basket. The young girls crooned, and a couple of boys stood shyly to the side until Meg invited them over so baby Jamin could clutch their finger tightly in his little fist.

Ben had organised someone from the gazette to come. They never had a wedding portrait taken, so they stood and posed for their family photograph. Meg looked so beautiful in the flush of motherhood. Ben stood there proudly looking over his son, his namesake. They had taken the last part of his name Benjamin, just as Liam was taken from the last part of William. It didn't hurt that the minister identified that Jamin was a Biblical name, a son of Simeon, which meant "right hand of favour." How appropriate was that.

After church the ladies brought out hampers to share lunch. The arrival of a baby was a big celebration. Tomorrow they go home.

Ben unfolded the letter and read it again. Meg sat in the easy chair, nursing Jamin. He grinned at his mother and twiddled with her braided hair as he nursed. Ben looked out the window and rubbed his lip thoughtfully. Meg pulled her eyes away from her son. "So, who's the letter from?"

"Liam."

"Oh? How are they going? Are the kids well?"

"Not sure. He doesn't mention them."

"Oh. Is everything okay? Why did he write?"

"Our grandmother died. He wrote this after the funeral. He said – it was… well, what you would expect of a Perkin's event."

"Oh Ben. I'm sorry you didn't get to go."

"I ain't too worried. We were never close. She was a hard woman with a hard way of doing life."

"I'm sorry…"

"Mum was more like Grandad in her way. But even then, it seemed we never got to know him well because Grandmother ruled the roost. She was formidable."

"That is so sad… to only have that sort of recollection of a person. Formidable doesn't seem like the most flattering memorial to leave your family."

"It fits her though." He looked out the window. "Liam said that the house on Perkins Road, has been jointly left to us. They would like to buy out our part of the property, if that is agreeable. They want to move there."

"Ben! They are coming? That is wonderful!"

He grinned. Yeah. It was. "I didn't even know the house was still in the family. Just assumed it had been sold. Liam reckons the bequest is probably a spiteful message of our unworthiness. When they read that part of the will, he said there were sniggers all around. No one even knew where Farthing is. The other property was split between her cousins and they were still squabbling over it like a pack of dogs with a bone when he left the reading. Typical… that Grandmother had to make a final dig at our illegitimacy."

"And yet… what appears to be intended as an insult, works out to be a blessing. They are going to move here!"

173

"Kind of fitting I guess that she has no idea this is the best possible outcome. Liam wants me to fix it up before they move in."

"Will they stay here while you work on it? I would love them to be close again."

"I was wondering… how would you feel about us converting the stone shed into a cottage and we stay down there. They can be in the house with the kids… just until the Perkin's Place is sorted. I'm not sure Ellen would be up to roughing-it just now… she's expecting again."

"She is?"

"Everyone crammed in here will be tight. I thought if we were there, it's close but we'd still have our own space and it'll be more settled for Jamin when he naps."

Meg walked around with Jamin for a moment until he squirmed from her arms and crawled away. "So, you are set on living in a shed again?"

"It's not big, but we could set it up nice enough. Not sure I could do Jensen and Eliza jumping on Jamin every morning before day-break. I think we are going to need our own space. Correction: I'm going to need it."

"It's an improvement on hessian dividers and packing case furniture. It probably won't burn down. How long will it take you to fix up the house?"

"The Perkin's Place hasn't been maintained. It was rented and some of the tenants were pretty rough. There's some significant work. I'm reckoning it'll take at least six months to do it properly. Should be able to have it done before their baby arrives."

Meg smiled. Her husband: the optimist. There was a very good chance his timeline was impossibly generous. After all, they had to set up the shed, move two families, maintain a business, work the farm. To have the renovations done by Christmas as well, especially if they hit complications or bad weather sounded overly confident to her. But that was fine. Her ambitions to have family around her son as he grew up, miraculously were again within reach. "Let's see what they think."

Ben put down the letter and pulled her into his arms. "Meg. The house where Jamin was born... that is the house."

"That old place? That is where your mother grew up? I thought you said it was a fine house."

"Well it probably was... twenty-five years ago."

"Huh. Why didn't you say so before?"

He shrugged. "It was more convenience than intention." It was not like he had connived to make it happen, but of the two available properties, he chose that one. And it did have a nice sense of symmetry. He felt close to his mum in those hours waiting to become a father. It was not hard to imagine her running through the rooms with dolls and skipping ropes in lace trimmed dresses and plaits with ribbons. Well, no one would ever run in a house governed by his grandmother. His mother had shown him a photo of her on the front stairs as a child, clutching a puppy that had belonged to the neighbour. She had been so excited that she was allowed to hold the puppy for the photograph. Ben grinned at the joke they shared: holding a puppy, even outside, was an unusual deviation from Grandmother's rules. Dignity and decorum were always the priority. It was agreeable to think that a new generation, with a different set of values would run through the hallways and talk love into the framework of that house.

Meg looked out the window towards the shed. The mosaicked walls shone in the sunlight in the beautiful earthen tones of the Petrea Downs stone. Already it had been show-cased to potential customers as a sample of the quarry product. Ahh, but now no longer just a shed, now a cottage: a small intimate home to share the privilege of family. She thought about every stone that Ben had laid; every conversation, every fight and kiss that those walls had witnessed in its short life. Each stone would now bear witness to many more years of loving and living. If only these walls could talk. If only they could write the story of the lives it would bear witness to in the future. What stories of healing it would tell!

More Stories by Olwyn Harris

Homes of Healing Series

#1 Beachside Cottage

 When beautiful, but naive, Eliza-Beth is led astray, rejected and ultimately disowned by her family, she finds herself face-to-face with Jensen Harker. Eliza-Beth's experience of men is that they are either weak, or callous. Jensen is different. Having recently lost his wife, he comes up with a plan to rescue Eliza-Beth. But will he be a man of his word? The family bible provides a catalyst for him to share his faith, and his life, with the troubled girl. Proving that redemption, healing, and acceptance can be found even in the most unusual or unexpected circumstances.

Gems of Australia; 6 Part Faith Series

#1 Sapphires of Hope

 Andi and Jo are best friends… they do pretty much everything together. So, when Andi has a catering assignment due, and only a tacky old basket to use, Jo helps her pull off the faded decorations, revealing a time-capsule of historical information, and in order to understand what it means, Andi and Jo ask their elderly neighbour to take them to visit the farm where the basket came from. They find themselves dumped back in history at the time of Federation, embroiled in circumstances that nearly cost Andi her life and threatens the livelihood of the people living there. How can they ever hope to keep going when things are spinning out of control?

Stand-alone Stories

Maggie & Minotaur

 Maggie Wick was shipped off to the city and high society life at the age of 12, where she would learn the way of the rich and marry into a family of influence. What could have caused her sudden return to Henderson's Gap? Can she really settle back into life on the station, with all its diversity and challenges? Will she find fulfilment in her role as a provisional schoolteacher? Will she ever figure out the "Captain", the mysterious, intimidating station manager?
When war comes to her little haven and Maggie's world comes crashing down, taking her loved ones and the Captain with it, Maggie needs to find a way to survive. Will her faith be enough to protect her, and what of the Captain? Could he really be the Theseus who would do battle with her Minotaur?

Matt's Boys of Wattle Creek.

 When Matthew Lawson's three sons were born, he wrote each of them a letter outlining his hopes and prayers for their futures. When he decided to give up his city job and move to the little town of Wattle Creek, he could never have imagined the effect it would have on his young family. As Matt's boys grow to maturity and find their places in their community, will his dreams and prayers come to fulfilment? Will his boys develop their own faith in the eternal God? And will they each find the kind of love that Matt holds for his beautiful Josie?

Coming Soon from Olwyn Harris

Homes of Healing Series
#3 The Writer's Retreat

The run-down stone cottage looked like the perfect place for Tess to retreat, not only to write her book but to escape her past. As she discovers her characters and delves into their stories, she also finds that God is delving into her own story at the same time. Her relationship with the local publican challenges her to stop running. Can she honestly confront the ugly aspects in her own story, so that God can bring them both to a place of healing?

Gems of Australia; 6 Part Faith Series
#2 Rubies of Ambition

Jo and Andi travel back into another period, this time with a beautiful actress named Lillian Browning from the 1920s who suddenly returns to the town of Gum Ridge where she grew up. The prickly-pear plague is at its height and desperation has invaded the hearts of people on all levels. How can Lillian find meaning outside her shattered ambitions? Will she ever reconnect with the people in her hometown who reject her pursuit of fame just like she rejected their humble community when she left?

#3 Emerald Dreams

Another time-warp journey finds Jo and Andi back in colonial times and they are horrified at the living conditions of those who had no choice but to live out the term of their natural life in Australia. Dreams seem a pointless exercise that belonged to their past. When the girls meet Polly, they start to see what is below the surface. Will Polly and her young daughter Jane, ever find a new way through the hardship to invest in their future dreams with anticipation?

Children's Books
Bush Olympics

A fun story that helps children understand that they have been uniquely created in God's sight. If the Bush Olympic coach, Mr Mopoke, can allow the animals to use their God-given talents and strengths, this wacky and wonderful team can go on to achieve great things.

www.ingramcontent.com/pod-product-compliance
Lightning Source LLC
Chambersburg PA
CBHW030430120726
47903CB00003B/896